Montana
Lawman

Marshal Reuben Hardin
Historical Westerns

Michael J Spanhanks

Publisher: Boggy Creek Press
Website: https://book.spanhanks.com/
Cover Design by Innovative Presentations

Cover Photography
Adobe Stock ID: 217729913

Bible References
Proverbs 3:5-6 (KJV)

A list of character can be found on the last page.

Forget About Kansas

*Sometimes you don't get to choose the trail.
It chooses you. —Unknown*

1

Marshal Reuben Hardin rode his gray Appaloosa, Amos, down the long, rugged hill. The journey from Kansas City had presented its challenges, but he could already smell the fresh air of higher elevation as he approached Miles City. He had crossed many rivers to reach this point, but sensed he was near Montana Territory, where he would begin his new position.

The rain during the early part of his trip had forced him to stop and pitch his tent near Powder River Ridge, where he had expected to encounter Arapaho and Cheyenne Indians almost anywhere along the trail. Instead, a small group of Chiricahua—a mix of various Apache tribes—maybe three or more, was tracking him, likely with the intent to steal his horse, weapons, and other items. They were undoubtedly waiting for the opportune moment to strike.

As he patted his horse on the side, he snorted. "Easy, boy," Hardin said, "we've got to keep going and find a safe spot to fend off these fellows." Turning the horse to scan the area, he wondered whether this group of Indians had found another path around him. Spotting no one following, he continued along the trail.

A few miles further, birds fluttered, and he pulled back the reins, quickly sliding from the saddle. Drawing his Henry repeating rifle from the scabbard, he tied Amos to a nearby tree. Carefully, he picked his way through the brush, stepping lightly until he caught a glimpse of movement in the sagebrush. Darting behind a large birch tree, he took off his hat as he noticed more movement to his left and then to his right. *They are spreading out.* He hoped his dark clothing would blend in with the forest colors and give him an advantage.

Hardin dropped to the ground when he saw one of them crawling toward Amos through the sage. *You can't have my horse.*

Thirty minutes passed, and they remained unmoved. Suddenly, one of them bounced from the ground and ran toward his horse. He raised his Henry Rifle and fired, knocking him to the ground. A noise caused him to turn. Another Indian was almost on top of him, with his hatchet in the air. Quickly, Hardin reached for his Colt and fired twice, hitting him in the chest and sending him to the Great Spirit. A paint horse sloshing through a creek about a hundred feet away confirmed the last of them was making his retreat.

Breathing a sigh of relief, Hardin rushed over to Amos and gave him a pat on the neck. "Boy, I don't think you would have liked it with them. Now, let's get this journey over with."

An hour later, Hardin came across a sign that read "Miles City." As he rode into town, he noticed a church at the far end with a tall steeple. To his right, wagons loaded with timber backed up to the mill. On the left side of the street, he spotted the train station. William Boyd, the Director of the U.S. Marshals Service, had mentioned that ranches in the area would one day use the train to transport their cattle to slaughterhouses east of the Mississippi River.

The town was bustling with activity—horses, wagons, and cowboys drifting in for supplies. Spotting the jail, Hardin brought Amos to a halt in front of the building and dismounted. Through an open door, he spotted a man leaning back in a chair, his boots resting on the desk, and a hat pulled down over his eyes. He took a few steps inside the office and noticed another man sprawled out asleep on a cot in a jail cell.

Hardin coughed and cleared his throat, keeping his eyes fixed on the man in the chair, who struggled to put his feet down and sit up straight. "I'm Marshal Reuben Hardin," he said.

"Erm, Bud Shepard, Sheriff," the man replied, rubbing his eyes. "Sorry, I must have dozed off. Yeah, the Director of the Marshal Services sent a telegram announcing you'd be coming."

Hardin extended his hand for a shake. "Glad to meet you, Sheriff. Boyd said you folks have some trouble in these parts. Was he wrong? You don't seem that busy," he said, taking a stab at the lawman's slothfulness.

"No, no, he wasn't," Shepard replied. "We've got our share of trouble—horse thieves, cattle rustlers, saloon fights; you name it."

"Maybe this job wears down one man."

"Two men," Shepard clarified. "The town pays for one extra man. Wade Norman pitches in when he can, but he mostly runs a leather shop. We handle our business."

"Would that be him in the jail asleep?" Hardin asked.

"Oh, no, got a drunkard in there sleeping it off."

"Un-huh?" Hardin replied with a piercing look.

"The town doesn't have funds for a full-time deputy. So, are you planning to stay in Miles City, Marshal?"

"I'll start here, but if my duties require me to be elsewhere regularly, I might need to reconsider my accommodations."

"I'm sure you'd like to know a little about our town, Marshal. The people are decent folks, though we do have a few unruly cowhands and travelers who pass through. Since the railroad came, it seems we've been dealing with more challenges than we've seen before. We can surely use you."

"I suppose those problems are a common theme with railroad towns."

"Well, maybe, but there's some good that came about with the railroad being here: we noticed a boost to our local businesses, and we've seen four or five new establishments come to town. Everyone thought at first we'd be simply a jerkwater town—you know, one of those quick stops for water, but then they built the station."

"Your town doesn't seem large enough to support a railroad, but I assume the location suited a purpose," Hardin reasoned. "Well, I should get settled in. Is there a hotel in town?"

"Yes, sir," Shepard responded. "We got a good one just a bit down the road on the right corner. You can't miss it."

Hardin looked out the door at Amos. "I also need a place for my horse."

"Just keep going past the hotel, and you'll see the livery most of the way down. There's no one better than Tobias Finch to take care of your horse."

"Thanks, Sheriff," Hardin said.

"Maybe I'll see you later in the hotel dining room. The food is pretty good," Shepard remarked.

Hardin gave a nod. "That sounds great—will be a chance to discuss where I should start."

Hardin stepped outside, mounted Amos, and rode toward the livery stable. Once he had taken care of his horse, he headed toward the hotel. The sign above the entrance, "Cactus Blossom Hotel," piqued his curiosity, as cacti didn't grow in the area.

A young woman in a yellow dress, about thirty, checked him in at the counter and handed him a key. Hardin nodded, then climbed the stairs and quickly located his room. Inside, there was a metal bed frame and a mattress, covered with a sheet and blanket. A picture of

President Lincoln hung on the wall. Next to the bed, a small wooden table held a white basin and a water pitcher. He set his belongings on the bed, then filled the basin with water and washed the dust off his arms and face.

Standing by the window, he could see the entire town, except for the street behind the hotel. He noticed a general merchandise store a few stores down.

He breathed out a sigh as he sat on the bed. A nap would certainly do him good, he thought, but perhaps he should arrange for someone to wake him in time for supper. Rising from the bed, he walked to the door. As he opened it, he spotted the woman from the front desk.

"Ma'am, would you mind knocking on my door before supper?" he asked.

She approached with a look of curiosity. "You want me to knock on your door? Sure. Maybe what you need is a little company, between now and supper."

Her response took him by surprise. "I didn't think this was a cathouse," Hardin remarked.

She looked at him with a playful smile. "It's not, but I can call the cats if you *really* need one."

"I'll keep that in mind, ma'am, but what I *need* right now is some rest."

The woman flashed him another grin. "Then by all means, sleep. I'll make sure you wake up at six."

"Thanks," Hardin said as she turned to leave. "Oh, wait a moment. What's your name?"

"Abigail," she replied, continuing to walk on.

"Beautiful name. Listen, I shouldn't be hard to wake," he added with a nod and a smile.

Abigail turned, walking backward toward the stairs, and responded, "Good, because I don't want to have to dump a bucket of water on you to rouse you. That might make the restaurant messy."

Hardin watched as she headed down the stairs. Once inside his room again, he hung his revolver and gun belt on an old wire tied at the head of the bed. Then, taking the weapon from its holster, he lay back down and soon fell asleep.

2

The aroma of food wafted up the stairs even before Abigail knocked on Hardin's door. He soon made his way to the restaurant, where he spotted Sheriff Shepard sitting at a table, sipping coffee.

As Hardin took a seat, Shepard declared, "I figured you'd be worn out from the trail and skip supper."

Hardin responded, shaking his head, "Nah, I'm a big man with a good appetite. So, what do they have to eat that's decent?"

"I've never had anything that wasn't favorable. I usually go for the special. Today, our owner, Eleanor Pike, is serving roast beef and potatoes with cornbread."

"Sounds perfect."

Sheriff Shepard stood from his seat, walked over to the waitress, ordered another special, and then returned to the table.

"Thank you," Hardin said.

Shepard offered a smile. "Well, hopefully, your food will arrive when mine does."

"Yeah. Uh, I was hoping to discuss some of the issues the territory is facing," Hardin said.

Sheriff Shepard turned his gaze away from the table, pondering the best guidance to give Hardin. "If you follow the river about twenty-five miles west, you'll find Bitterroot Springs. There's been some trouble between the timber cutters there and a rancher named Cornelius Vance. The timber folks cut his trees and hauled them to the mill for lumber. Vance was to receive payment once they had milled them down, and was expected to pay them. A newspaper article from Bitterroot mentioned that Vance received payment but didn't bother to share it with them. It also said because of that, a gunfight could happen between Vance and the timber crew."

"Doesn't this town, Bitterroot, have a sheriff to handle this?" Hardin inquired.

"Marshal, you'll find that many of the small and mid-sized towns have no law. Their man died in a fight, or they can't find anyone willing to take the job. Most towns rely on the army."

"All of Montana needs law and order—I suppose it's why they sent a marshal. I figure the territory will apply for stateship directly."

"I reckon you're right, but then, not every man is suited to be a lawman," Shepard said, "which is why this wilderness attracts criminals and other no-goods."

The waitress brought their food and drinks and set them on the table. "Is there anything else, gentlemen?" she asked.

"No, that will be all, Clara," Shepard responded, turning his attention again to Hardin.

"Sheriff, you mentioned a newspaper article. Which newspaper?" Hardin asked.

"The Bitterroot Chronicle—the onliest one they have. A woman named Sarah Harlan runs it. Took it over from her father, Horace, when he died."

"It's uncommon to see a woman writing stories of controversy and putting her life in danger."

"Out here, Marshal, there are plenty of women carving their own paths around dangerous situations. In most towns, bordellos cater to women who can't find work."

"I suppose that's true most everywhere," Hardin said as he took a bite of food.

"Does the meal suit you?"

"I've had worse."

"Yeah, me too," Shepard remarked. "The food in the army was terrible. We thought we'd done gone to heaven if we could eat in a town once in a while. What about you? You serve in the military?"

"The Civil War," Hardin replied. "Our food often came to us spoiled. My Lieutenant sent out our sharpshooters to hunt for whatever they could kill and bring safely back."

"I never served in the Civil," Shepard said. "Did my time as a Buffalo Soldier at Fort Atkinson. Our task was to protect the settlers from the Indians and maintain order on the plains. What a job that was! I barely came out of it alive, though I suppose being so deep in it is why I became a sheriff. What about you?" he asked, taking another bite of food.

Hardin set his fork aside. "After the war, I became a Pony Express Rider, until they asked us to ride through the badlands. I came across moose, elk, and mountain lions, which weren't too bad. It was all those grizzlies that drove me back to the Midwest. After that, I worked for a while for a ranch in Kansas, and then I thought I might try my hand at being a sheriff in a town called Hays City. The town was wild as ever with outlaws and gunfighters riding through constantly when I first took the job."

"Those were terrible times," Shepard said.
"So, what else needs a lawman's attention? William Boyd didn't send me just to handle a skirmish between some rancher and timbermen."

"Well, they been some cattle rustling happening—some say Rufus Hale's gang's behind it, but I don't know that," responded Shepard. "Nobody's ever caught them red-handed and lived to tell it."

"So you got rustlers who turned to murder-ing?" Hardin asked.

"At a campfire in Wolf Hollow, they found two men dead—the branding iron was still hot."

Shepard's story reminded Hardin of a gang he ran across in Kansas years ago, who didn't hesitate to kill if it meant they could keep rustling cattle and rebranding for profit. Eight men, mostly small ranchers, lost their lives in just six months before the gang was caught and hanged. "Rustling always seems to spiral out of control," he added.

"Well, I might as well tell you now," Shep-ard said. "There are several large ranches in Montana—all cattle barons—who own land around Miles City. There are a few at Bitter-root, too. Each is determined to own the others' cattle and land. I expect a range war to break out someday. No one can predict when."

Hardin pushed his plate back. "Thanks for sharing this with me, Sheriff. First thing I'll do after I get some rest is head out to Bitterroot Springs to see if I can make some progress on this timber feud."

"Well, good luck, Marshal."

"I'll come by your office early. Could you have a list of the cattle ranchers' names and the woman who wrote the article you mentioned ready? I will look her up, too. Could be she has more information to share."

"Sure, Marshal. Now, I'm heading over to the saloon to check on things. Can I buy you a drink?"

"I don't partake in the brew," Hardin replied.

"I've never known a lawman to turn down a cold beer," Shepard remarked with an odd grin.

"Well, now you do. I've seen too much ruin caused by the drink in my family, plus I'm a man of faith."

Shepard's brows furrowed. "How does your faith align with this job? There'll surely be times when you'll have to take a life in the line of duty. Doesn't the Good Book prohibit killing?" he asked.

"You're talking about murder. If you read the Good Book, you'd know sometimes men die for the sake of justice on the side of the law and not."

"Sounds like a grey area to me."

"Not if you're living right. A man of faith should always be aware of what's right and wrong."

"I hope that principle serves you well in Montana," Shepard said, "but I have a feeling you're going to reconsider it."

Hardin stood up from the table and laid down money to cover his meal. "I won't. I'll see you in the morning."

"I'll be there," Shepard replied.

3

After having breakfast at the restaurant the following morning, Marshall Hardin saddled Amos, collected the list of names that Sheriff Shepard had promised, and set out for Bitterroot Springs.

The road was fairly smooth as he rode alongside the Powder River. On the opposite side of the trail were grazing lands for both large and small ranchers, as well as woods. You could tell the size of the ranches by the number of hands working the herds. By the end of the day, Hardin had crossed three creeks before realizing some weariness in Amos and brought him to a stop.

"Okay, boy, let's camp here," Hardin said. "There's no sense in trying to reach Bitterroot before dark when there are plenty of good spots along the river."

The sky was clear as he removed Amos' saddle and set it on the ground. He tied the horse to a long rope and offered him a few handfuls of grain. "Eat this, and I'll get you some water."

He gathered an armful of dry wood and some brush for kindling and squatted to build a campfire. Once the flames took hold, Hardin walked back into the woods for more dry branches to help keep the fire going through the night.

He reached for a branch when he heard a limb snap nearby. "Who's there?" he called out.

"Just me, pilgrim," came the reply, as a man stepped out from the woods. He was clad in clothes made of deer skin, sported a gray beard, and carried a Hawken Black Powder rifle. A large imitation Jim Bowie fixed-blade knife hung from his belt, and a bulging pouch of furs draped over his shoulder.

"State your business," Hardin said, eyeing the newcomer warily.

"Just passing through and smelled your campfire. I was wondering if I might settle here tonight," the man said.

Hardin took a moment to size him up before responding. "Sure, feel free to drop your things near the fire."

After gathering a second load of dry wood, Hardin returned to camp and dropped it beside the fire. Wiping the dirt from his hands, he turned to the stranger. "What's your name?"

"Silas Granger. I trap this timberland along the river," the man replied.

"So, Silas, do you have a home?" Hardin inquired.

"Sort of," Silas replied. "I took over an old cabin about fifteen years ago, but then a storm came through and lifted off part of the roof. So when I'm not trapping or hunting, I cut logs to build a new one. I hope to have it finished by winter, but if not, I'll manage as I did last year. I stayed on one side of the old cabin and put up a canvas to block the cold from the damaged part."

"That's lots of work for a man getting along in years."

"I may be growing older, but I'm not scared of hard work," Silas remarked with a bit of pride in his voice.

"I didn't mean to imply that," Hardin said, leaning to add another branch to the fire.

Silas caught a glimmer of the badge peeking from behind the marshal's vest. "I didn't picture you as a lawman."

"Oh? Why's that?" Hardin asked, raising an eyebrow.

"You're clean-shaven, okay, but there's a ruggedness to your face that might make someone mistake you for an outlaw without that badge," Silas remarked with a slight grin.

As they sat staring at the flames, Silas produced a rabbit that had already been skinned and cleaned. "How about we roast this hare over the fire?" he suggested. "Help yourself and consider it payment for the use of your campfire."

Hardin regarded the trapper with a furrowed brow. "I'd never ask you to pay."

"Oh, I figured as much," the trapper replied with a big smile, exposing a missing tooth.

"Thanks. I'll find a limb to make a spit and get it cooking," Hardin said.

As he positioned the meat over the flame, Silas reached into his clothing and pulled out a small bottle of spirits, taking a swig. "Mmm, here, have a drink, Pilgrim," he offered.

"Nah, I'd rather not," Hardin replied politely.

"You're not a drinking man?" the trapper inquired.

"Only coffee and water for me."

"If you keep marshaling in these parts, you might just find yourself turning to drink," Silas remarked with a serious tone.

"Why's that?"

"There's plenty of trouble around here. The towns are more than one marshal can handle. Of course, you could always summon the army."

"Tell me about the trouble when I get back," Hardin said.

"Where are you headed now?"

"To the river. I need to water my horse."

Silas attended to the rabbit on the spit as Hardin untied Amos and led him toward the river. After a short while, he returned, rubbing down the horse with a rag from his saddlebags before tying him out again.

"Silas, you don't ride a horse or mule?" Hardin inquired as he made his way back to the fire.

"I had a mule once, but it turned out to be a lot of trouble. They need grain, but how do I give that to 'em when I'm deep in the woods trapping?"

Hardin gave an understanding nod. "Yeah, you have to take care of them if you're gonna own one."

"Marshal, how long have you been in Montana?" the trapper asked curiously.

"About a week."

"Yeah, that's what I figured. You're a greenhorn to the territory. You still don't know about all the trouble that goes on, Marshal."

"I'm aware of some of it, but tell me what you mean?" Hardin urged.

"I hear there's some huge misunderstanding regarding payment for timber work at Bitterroot," Silas explained. "Those fellows are liable to stir up a fight."

"I'm actually on my way to Bitterroot Springs now. Sheriff Shepard in Miles City gave me the heads-up already," Hardin said.

Silas looked away, stroking his beard with his fingers. Turning back to Hardin, he continued, "I know lawmen often associate, Marshal, but you need to hear me out about Shepard. Word is, he's as much a criminal as any known in these parts."

"Please elaborate," Hardin prompted.

Silas gazed intently at Hardin. "I've heard Sheriff Shepard has cowboys hired on to rustle cattle for him. He gives them a reasonable percentage of the sales from their work." Silas looked down at the ground and then back at Hardin, adding, "Are you as crooked as Sheriff Shepard, Marshal?"

"With confidence, I can say that I am not," Hardin replied. "Silas, are you certain about all of this?"

"Around some, it's common knowledge. I'm warning you—Shepard will try to twist the facts to hide his corruption."

"I appreciate you bringing it to my attention, Silas."

"Marshal, do you think you can do something about it, being just one man?"

"Maybe. First, I have to gather evidence," Hardin replied. "Once I have that, I'll take it to Fort Keogh. I'm sure the Army would be willing to assist. In the meantime, maybe I should ride to the fort and introduce myself."

"I hope that works out for you. Be careful—the soldiers might be in cahoots with Sheriff Shepard."

Hardin reflected on Silas's remarks, wondering if the soldiers might really be involved in cattle rustling. His gaze fixated on the meat, uncertainty swirling in his mind. "I believe this meat is done," Hardin said, ignoring the trapper's last comment. "Let me carve you off some."

"You first, since it's my treat," Silas replied, feeling generous.

After they had eaten, the two men settled down on the ground and fell asleep.

Hardin awakened the next morning to the smell of coffee. He propped himself up and saw Silas pouring some into a tin cup.

"I noticed your pack there on the ground," Silas remarked. "Hope you don't mind that I made coffee. Never touched your other things—I'm not a thief."

"That's fine," Hardin replied. "Coffee is the one thing I always bring, even if I don't have food."

Silas held up another tin cup. "I also found this in your things. Let me pour you a cup."

"I appreciate it, Silas."

Hardin took a few sips of coffee before standing up and stretching out the stiffness that had settled on him from sleeping on the ground. He then sat on a log beside Silas, his gaze turning to his horse. "I need to get Amos some water before I leave."

"Where did you come up with the name for that horse?" Silas asked curiously.

"He had the name when I bought him. The woman who sold him to me had lost her husband and said the horse was named after an old mule his father once owned. I didn't see the need to change it," Hardin explained.

"Well, it works. Marshal, after I finish this cup, I think I'll mosey along. I've got a few traps set nearby that I should check before heading west."

"Silas, could you do me a favor?"

"What do you need?" the trapper questioned.

"If you make it into town or run into your fur buyers, keep an ear out for news about outlaws, bandits, shootings, cattle rustlers, and the like," Hardin declared, reaching into his pocket to hand Silas a few dollars. "I hope this shows that I trust you. If you hear anything related to these, I'd appreciate it if you could send me a telegram. I'll be at Bitterroot Springs for a few days, then I'll head back to Miles City."

"Oh, sure, Marshal, I'll do that," Silas replied, reaching for the money. "I hope you can clean up this territory."

"Maybe you should code any telegrams," Hardin suggested. "I don't need the telegraph operator knowing my business. Use my name, then you might say something like, 'Got what you need. Meet me at...' and you choose the location."

"Yeah, sounds easy enough. Sometimes I sell furs at Miles City—I might try to meet you there if I know anything."

"And how far is it from here to Bitter-root?" Hardin inquired.

"I'd estimate about fifteen more miles."

"Thanks for the rabbit," Hardin said, nodding appreciatively.

"Yeah, we'll share another meal someday, but I need to get to my traps."

"I'll see you around."

As the older man walked into the woods and disappeared from view, it reminded Hardin of another man Silas resembled, Sid Hartford. Sid ran a freighter outfit out of Kansas City, a dedicated worker who frequently encountered Indians and thieves, yet always emerged unscathed. Until one fateful day, he took a bullet and drew his last breath, passing while doing what he loved. Hardin wondered if Silas might one day meet a similar end along the trails he hunted and trapped, and years would pass before anyone realized it.

After taking Amos for water, Hardin saddled him, secured his gear, and set off for Bitterroot Springs.

4

The town of Bitterroot Springs exuded a peaceful calm as Hardin rode in. He surveyed the names of the businesses along the street and finally came to the newspaper building. Its frontage featured a door midway, and windows displaying the words "Bitterroot Chronicle" along with the smaller inscription "Susan Harlan, Journalist/Proprietor."

Hardin dismounted in front of the building, dusted himself off, and tied Amos to a hitch rail. He then stepped onto the porch and entered the business. Inside, a large desk lined one wall, a printing machine stood across from it, and shelves at the back held stacks of paper. Cans labeled "ink" were neatly arranged, ready for use.

No one responded to Hardin's call, so he sat at the desk and gazed out the window. As he observed the businesses and the people moving about, he realized Bitterroot was simply a smaller version of Miles City. To his surprise, the small town boasted two banks directly across from each other on the main street, as if they were rivals.

Suddenly, the door swung open, and a young woman with brunette hair, wearing a pink dress, stood there staring at him. "Who are you?" she asked.

"Marshal Reuben Hardin, I'd like to ask you a few questions about the article you wrote a few days ago."

"What article? I write a lot of articles," she replied.

"You are Sarah Harlan?" the marshal asked.

"Yes, that's me. I run the printing shop and deliver papers."

"Do you recall an article you wrote about the dispute between some timbermen and a rancher?"

"Of course I do."

"I'm interested in the details you might not have printed or were hesitant to include."

"Marshal, I'm not sure what you're refer-ring to," Sarah replied as she approached a coat rack and removed her shawl.

"I don't want to cause you any trouble, ma'am, and I might not be asking properly. I realize..."

"Sir, I have to be somewhere right now," Sarah interrupted, walking toward the door. "Perhaps I'll see you later." She pushed open the door and hurried down the board-walk.

Frustrated, Hardin mounted his horse and rode through town until he spotted the Lone-some Pine Café, where he pulled back the reins. "Wait out here, Amos. I'm not sure how long this will take."

Amos snickered, which brought a smile to Hardin's face. "Sometimes I think you know what I'm saying."

He walked through the door, spotted a small table, and sat down. While waiting for a wait-ress, he scanned the room and noticed Sarah Harlan, the journalist, sitting at a table with a man in a suit. The waitress came to take their order and then brought them some drinks.

Hardin noticed her hand on the table, reaching out to the young man.

"Sir, do you know what you'd like to order?" a voice suddenly interrupted, drawing his attention back.

"I apologize," Hardin replied. "What's the special today?"

"We have a pot of chili served with cornbread," she answered. "The sweet tea is always a favorite."

"All of that sounds great to me," he said.

"I'll bring your tea right away. We're waiting on another pan of cornbread to come out of the oven," she said with a smile.

"That's fine," he replied.

Hardin watched as the blond waitress, about his age, made her way back to the kitchen.

She soon set his tea on the table, and after about ten minutes, returned with his food. "Here you go. That wasn't too long, was it?"

"Perfect," he responded.

"You're new in town, aren't you?" she asked.

"Just rode in."

"Got a name?"

Hardin grinned. "Reuben Hardin, Marshal Reuben Hardin."

"I'm Lydia," she said, noticing the badge. "Well, Marshal, I hope you'll stay for a while."

"I won't be in town long," he said, tearing a piece of cornbread in two. "I've got a little business, and then I'll head back to Miles City."

"That's unfortunate, Marshal. I was hoping you might take me on a picnic and I could fill you in on crimes I hear talked about," she said, a grin spreading across her face as she turned to walk away. While still in earshot, she spun around and said, "Oh, I almost forgot—the meal is fifty cents."

Hardin nodded and took a bite of his chili. The waitress checked with him several times to see if he needed anything else. Just as he was about to leave, a man wearing a suit sat down across from him.

"I noticed you were a lawman from over at my table, and now that I'm sitting in front of you, I see you're a U.S. Marshal—that's wonderful. I'm Glenn Barlow, the Mayor of Bitterroot Springs."

"I'm glad to meet you, Mr. Barlow," Hardin said. "What can I do for you?"

"Well, I was hoping to persuade you to settle here in Bitterroot," Barlow said.

"Mayor, it's difficult to say where I'll make my home. At the moment, I'm still familiarizing myself with the territory," Hardin replied.

"We have fine people in our town, but we truly need the presence of a lawman," Barlow added.

"Why not hire someone as sheriff?"

"We've made attempts, believe me. Unfortunately, the only candidates willing to accept the position have questionable backgrounds."

"I'm sorry, Mr. Barlow. I can't make any promises. Someday I might feel the need to be closer to your town, but for now, I'll be residing in Miles City."

"At least we know you'll be accessible if we require your assistance. Thank you for your time, Marshal," Barlow said, standing to leave.

"Hold on a moment. Before you go, can you provide any information about this squabble between the timber folks and a rancher named Cornelius Vance?" Hardin asked.

"Sure," Barlow replied, taking a seat across from Hardin. "Most of the town is upset with Vance over this situation. Ever since he arrived, he's caused nothing but trouble. He purchased a significant amount of land and brought in cattle from Kansas to get started."

"As I understand it, Vance had these timber workers cut and haul timber from his land to the mill," Hardin shared. "The mill pays him, but he refuses to compensate the timber workers for their share."

"That's correct, Marshal. The payment rules for the mill were established before my time as mayor, because the timber workers were worried about possible cheating by the mill. To avoid problems, the mill decided to pay the landowner directly for their timber."

"That seems entirely counterintuitive."

"You're probably right. I tried to persuade the mill to revert to the old system," Barlow replied.

"The best way to resolve the feud is for the mill to split the payment," Hardin suggested.

"I don't think they'll ever agree to that after what happened, but you're welcome to try. We hadn't faced payment issues with the cutters until Cornelius Vance showed up. Let me tell you about him: Vance employs several cowboys, all of whom carry guns on their hips. I've heard that two of them are professional gunmen. What kind of person hires gunslingers?" Barlow asked.

"The kind of man who needs a lot of protection or one who intends to push people around."

Barlow nodded in agreement. "Exactly my thoughts."

"What can you tell me about these timbermen?" Hardin asked.

"There are about a dozen of them," Barlow replied, "but three seem in charge, with one having the final say on which land they cut timber from. His name is Josiah Reed. The other two are Duncan Malloy and Caleb Warrick. All of these men, along with the other cutters, are quite sturdy and tend to come out on top in a fight."

"What about firearms, Mayor? Do any of them carry weapons?"

"They don't use holsters and sidearms, if that's what you're asking, Marshal. But everyone in this territory has a weapon and knows how to use it—shotguns, black powder guns, and rifles. There are still renegade Indians roaming the area."

"I think I'll ride out there and meet the timber people."

"Who you really should talk to is her," Barlow suggested, gesturing toward Sarah Harlan. "Sarah stirred up quite a bit of trouble with an article. I'm shocked someone hasn't come after her. The mill, the timber folks, and Vance were all quite upset with her."

"I stopped by the printing shop to see her, but she seemed in quite a rush to get away."

"Jonathan Starks is courting Sarah," Barlow said, staring at the back of the head of the young man wearing the suit. "He works at one of the banks. They've been seeing each other for a while now."

"That's the other thing I noticed about this town. Are two banks really necessary?"

"Definitely not. A man named Amos Cutler, another prominent rancher, sought a loan to bring in a herd of longhorns from Texas, but Gideon Holt, the owner of the original bank, turned him down. That decision didn't sit well with Amos. He had friends from back east willing to fund the establishment of another bank, and this move hurt Gideon Holt."

"Sounds like another feud brewing," Hardin remarked.

"Could be, Marshal, and I believe this one will likely end up in court."

"By the way, when does the judge come around these parts?"

"I'm afraid we never see the judge since we don't have a sheriff. For any legal matters, we have to take them to Miles City. Judge Shelton Quinn has an office and a courtroom there. You'll likely see him for warrants. Well, look at the time—I'd better head home. Please consider what I asked you, Marshal."

"Alright, but I can't make any promises."

Barlow turned and walked out the door.

As Hardin stood to leave, he noticed Sarah Harlan watching and sneering at him.

5

After a night's rest at the Drifter's Hotel, Hardin headed to the livery to get his horse. He led Amos into a hallway and tossed his saddle on him. While tightening the girth, two men appeared on the other side of the horse.

"Marshal, we're glad to see you in Bitterroot, but we could really use your help," said a man wearing brown trousers held up by dark blue suspenders. His face was unshaven, and he wore a sullied buff-colored hat.

"Hardin's my name—and you are?" he asked, his eyes fixed on them.

"Duncan Malloy," the man replied, extending his hand over Amos to shake Hardin's.

The second man grasped the marshal's hand and said, "My name's Caleb Warrick."

"What can I help you fellows with?" Hardin inquired.

"Two weeks ago, we cut timber for a man named Cornelious Vance," Duncan explained. "Vance got his payment from the mill. Now, it's customary for the owner of the timber to pay the cutters for their work, but Vance believes he can dodge paying us."

Hardin sighed and walked around his horse. "Men, I'm willing to look into your situation, but I can't force the man to pay you. I will, however, apply pressure to honor his commitment."

"Marshal, our whole crew lost money on that deal," Caleb said. "Most of the men have families, and times are tough. If you can't get our money from Vance, we'll take matters into our own hands."

"Now listen here, men," Hardin replied. "If I were in your position, I'd steer clear of Vance. He has plenty of firepower on hand. I don't know him yet, but you seem outmatched."

Duncan frowned and said, "No, Marshal, we aren't outmatched. Every tree cutter in our camp is armed and knows how to use it."

"Duncan, Caleb, I'd advise you to reconsider that idea," Hardin continued, "unless you have a few gunhands on your side, because Vance certainly does. Men like him employ hired guns for situations just like this. Do yourselves a favor next time you negotiate a timber deal—get it in writing. Have an attorney draft a contract and make sure both the landowner and the mill sign it. Now, I've got work to attend to. You gentlemen should head back to your camp."

"Marshal, this ain't over," Duncan said firmly as the two men turned to leave the stables.

Hardin shook his head as he guided his horse toward the door.

Ezra Tate, the stableman, approached after finishing up in a stall. "Marshal, it sounds like those two are going to be trouble for you," he remarked.

"But I can't arrest them until they actually commit a crime," Hardin responded.

"Yeah, well. So, are you planning to be gone overnight?" Ezra asked.

Hardin mounted Amos and glanced over at Ezra. "I hope to finish this job in half a day."

"Would you like a bit of grain in case you're out longer, Marshal?" Ezra offered.

After a moment of consideration, Hardin replied, "Yes, please get me enough for overnight."

Ezra quickly grabbed a small cloth sack, filled it with grain, and handed it to Hardin. He secured it in his saddlebags, turned to bid Ezra farewell, and rode away.

Dust swirled through the air as Grant Walls brought his mare to a stop at the ranch house and tied her to the hitch rail. Stepping inside, he saw Vance seated at his desk.

"Did you get those mama cows moved?" Vance asked.

"Rowdy and Joe are working on that now, boss. We had to finish branding the calves," Grant responded.

"Make sure they don't take long—that watering hole is nearly bone dry."

"We definitely need rain in the worst way."

"It's like this every year until the fall. We'll get more than our share of rain when the time's right, followed by lots of snow," Vance said, glancing toward the door.

"Hey, boss, there's a rider coming down the lane," Abner Cole remarked. "He looks like a lawman."

"How can you tell?" Vance asked.

"I'm not sure. Maybe it's the way he sits in the saddle. There's something serious about his demeanor."

"Tell him I'll be out shortly," Vance replied.

Abner nodded and made his way toward the door.

"Why do you reckon a lawman is coming here, boss? Grant asked.

"How should I know?" Vance replied. "We'd better find out. I'll handle this—you go find Micah and Wesley and have them stand by with their guns ready."

Out front, Hardin dismounted as he waited for the rancher. He looked around at Vance's operation while the elder Abner leaned against the porch.

Moments later, the door swung open, and an older man—graying, partially bald, and sporting a mustache—stepped out, dressed in blue trousers and suspenders. At the same time, Hardin noticed another man hurrying off the porch and heading toward the barn.

Vance gazed at Hardin and walked to the edge of the porch. Hardin removed his hat and extended his hand to shake. The older man hesitated for a moment before finally presenting his hand to shake. "Cornelius Vance. How can I help you, lawman?"

Hardin's peripheral vision caught three men strolling towards the porch. One was the same man who had left earlier, while the other two, he thought, were hired gunhands. "I'm U.S. Marshal Reuben Hardin, and I'd like to discuss the trees the timbermen recently cut from your property. They claim you cheated them out of their share of the sales. What's your response?"

"That timber bunch has been complaining for a week, claiming I defrauded them," Vance replied. "But they have no proof. Marshal, it's simply my word against theirs."

"So, did you... defraud them?" Hardin asked. When no response came, he added. "Vance, I'm new to this area. You, however, have to live with the people of this territory. If you've swindled those men, I can assure you it will come back to bite you."

"Lawman, I go by my own laws," Vance replied coolly. "If the government truly wanted the rule of law in these parts, it would have set it up long ago. Most of the towns have no sheriffs. When one of the so-called good citizens cheated me out of some cattle I already paid him for, I realized I could no longer trust folks from around here. I brought in my own law, Marshal." He turned and gestured toward his gunhands. "Those timbermen should learn how to conduct their business properly, or they'll find themselves going broke."

"Vance, that might be true, but it doesn't negate the fact that the timbermen have accused you of stealing money from them."

The rancher perked up like a rooster and hooked his thumbs through his suspenders. "What are you going to do about it, Marshal?"

Hardin took a deep breath and slowly exhaled. "This is just a warning, Vance. The army is only a few miles away, and it wouldn't be difficult to enlist their help if necessary."

"You go ahead and try that, Lawman, and you'll see what kind of war you'll be facing."

One of the gunmen reached for his weapon, but Hardin was faster, firing a bullet into the man's hand.

"Wesley, that wasn't necessary!" Vance shouted, turning to the wounded gunman and shaking his head in frustration. "Grant, get him inside and tend to his hand."

As Grant hurried to assist the injured gunfighter, Vance turned his gaze back to Hardin. "Are you going to be trouble for me, Marshal?"

"I didn't reach for my gun until your man did," Hardin replied.

"Yeah, I know, and I apologize for that. It seems these young guns don't use their noggin," Vance remarked. Then he turned and faced Hardin directly, his eyes on the marshal's weapon. "Marshal, I'll talk to the tim-bermen and see if we can settle it. Maybe we can avoid a conflict."

"I hope you mean it," Hardin replied as he mounted his horse.

"When you see those timbermen, let them know I'll be by to see them," Vance remarked.

"Sure." With that, Hardin turned his horse and rode away.

6

As dawn broke the next morning, Hardin saddled his horse and headed to the Lonesome Pine Café just up the street. He stepped inside and bought a biscuit and some bacon for his journey.

A few miles from Bitterroot Springs, he came across a wagon being pulled by four horses. As he drew closer, he greeted the man and said, "Hello there."

"Howdy," came the gruff reply. "I've got only a few items in the wagon."

"Just being friendly," Hardin said. "I'm a U .S. Marshal. Have you run into any trouble in these parts?"

"Name's Grover French, and I'm a freighter heading back to Miles City. Haven't seen any trouble today."

"Mr. French, where do you get supplies?" Hardin asked.

"Glendive Cantonment is my supply depot. Goods come in by steamboat when the river permits. Once the railroad gets underway—I'm not sure when that will be—they'll set up a new pickup location. It might be at Glendive, but that's still up in the air."

"Glendive Cantonment is quite a distance from here, isn't it?" Hardin inquired.

"Yes, sir, seventy-five miles, but it feels like a hundred bouncing on this wagon seat," Grover French replied.

"Are there any Indians in the area?"

"You know...."

Before Grover could finish his sentence, an arrow whistled through the air and embedded in the side of the wagon.

"Get down, Mr. French!" Hardin shouted.

As French grabbed his rifle and dropped to the ground, Hardin quickly maneuvered Amos behind the wagon, away from the arrow's direction. After dismounting and securing the horse to the wagon, Hardin drew his rifle from its scabbard.

"What kind of Indians are in this area?" Hardin asked.

"The only ones I've heard about around here are the Nez Perce," French replied. "I wonder what they want?"

Hardin peered around the edge of the wagon, scanning the woods on the opposite side of the road. He spotted two braves. "I see two of them wearing war paint."

"There's another one on this side," French added.

"What do you have inside the wagon, Mr. French?"

French's eyebrow shot up as he turned to Hardin. "Only got a small bag of sugar, a fifty-pound bag of meal flour, and a case of whisky. But *they're* not getting any of it!"

Hardin slipped him a stern look. "Would you rather they take the supplies, or your scalp? I've heard reports of Indians raiding ranches and farms for food. I don't see any horses, so they either walked here or have them tied out of sight. They can't carry much by hand. Just give them a couple of bags."

"I can't start doing that, Marshal, or they might all take advantage," French replied, shaking his head.

"Yes, that's a risk, but it favors them. Either give it to them, or I will," Hardin insisted.

Grover French's face reddened with anger as he climbed into the wagon from the rear. A moment later, he poked his head out, holding up a twenty-pound bag of sugar.

One of the Indians, a commanding figure, approached them, seemingly satisfied with the gesture. He held a rifle in one hand, with a hatchet and knife hanging from his waist. Colored bands adorned his arms, and streaks of black paint marked his face, creating a fearsome appearance.

Hardin stepped out from behind the wagon, startling the man. The Indian halted in his tracks, but Hardin motioned for him to come forward. "I will not shoot. Take it."

The Indian eyed him as he drew closer. "We not go to reservation," he stated. "We go to Grandmother's Country soon, you call Canada, where no soldiers live."

"I understand," Hardin replied. "If you ask for food along the way, I believe that people will gladly help you."

The Indian paused for a moment. "We will not forget."

"What's your name?"

"Nayati."

"Mr. French, give Nayati and his friends that sack of flour," Hardin instructed.

Grover looked at Hardin in disbelief. "Give them a sack of flour? What will they do for me?"

The large Indian responded, "When you drive wagon through trail, we will fight the Comancheros with you."

"There are Comancheros this far north?" Hardin asked.

"Many tribes journey to Grandmother's Country to be free from soldiers and settlers," the Indian explained. "The Comancheros not have tribe. They Mexican, Pueblo, Apache, Navajo. They rob and trade—some murder."

As French dragged the bag of flour to the back, the Indian motioned for one of his warriors to come forward. They accepted the sugar and flour and disappeared into the woods.

"Marshal, I don't know if you did me a favor or not," French remarked. "Can I trust that he'll keep his word?"

"He seemed sincere to me," Hardin replied. "You can only hope he does."

Grover French climbed into his wagon and set his horses on the trail as Hardin rode around him.

The sergeant shouted an order, calling the soldiers to the formation drill. The army had designed the exercise to prepare the unit for effective maneuvers during encounters with Native American tribes.

As the soldiers carried out the drills, the gate creaked opened, and a rider urged his horse toward the office. A soldier greeted him at the hitch rails as he slowed the gelding.

"I'd like to speak with the Colonel, if I may," Marshal Hardin requested.

"Just a moment while I check with him," the soldier replied.

Hardin secured Amos to a hitch rail and waited beside him while the soldier stepped inside.

A few moments later, the soldier returned. "Colonel Miles will see you. This way, please."

Hardin followed him through one room to another, where he spotted a man with slicked-back hair and a mustache, seated behind a desk and wearing a uniform decorated with medals.

The Colonel looked up at him. "You're a lawman, I understand. How may I assist you?"

"Is your name Colonel Miles?" Hardin asked.

"It is."

"I'm U.S. Marshal Reuben Hardin, and I'll be working in this territory, Colonel."

"This is quite a large area for one lawman. Are there others coming to help you?" the Colonel inquired.

"Not to my knowledge. I just wanted to inform you that I'll be around, should you need assistance."

"That's good to know. Perhaps I can offer *you* a favor, Marshal. I understand that Miles City has a jail, but if you need extra space for prisoners, we have facilities here at the fort."

"Thank you, Colonel. While I'm here, I'd also like to inquire if you've heard about a dispute involving some timber workers and a rancher."

"You must mean Cornelius Vance," Colonel Miles replied. "The man has been in this territory for only about a year and has already built a name for not getting along with others."

"That's him."

"What's he done this time?"

"It seems he had some timber cut from his property by a group of cutters who have a camp outside of Bitterroot Springs. The Bitterroot mill compensated Vance for the entire run, but he hasn't paid the men who did the tree cutting and hauling."

"Sounds like Vance. Do you want us to bring him in?" Colonel Miles asked.

"No, I just visited Vance. Our conversation led me to believe he might go ahead and pay them. I prefer to give it some time to see if this resolves itself."

"I hope you're right, Marshal, but knowing Vance, I have my doubts."

"You think he lied to me?"

"Maybe not outright, but he certainly doesn't have a reputation for honesty, that much is certain."

"How do you know so much about a rancher who's forty miles away?" Hardin asked.

"About a year ago, a man living north of Miles City bought some cattle from Vance to start a small ranch. I'm not sure how it started, but one night, the rancher grabbed Vance by the neck and cornered him against the wall outside the saloon. Who knows what might have happened if a few of my soldiers hadn't come by and intervened? We learned from the rancher what Vance had done."

"Colonel, I think Vance mentioned the incident. It seems this prompted him to hire some gunhands. Although he assured me he would talk to the timber cutters to resolve the issue, I know he doesn't employ gunhands to herd cattle."

"Now that's troubling."

"Yes, it is," Hardin said with a sigh. "There's something else I need to ask. Have you heard anything about cattle rustling in the area?"

"I certainly have, Marshal. You should speak with a man named Nathaniel Boone. He had twenty heads stolen about a month ago. While he couldn't be entirely sure, he thought he spotted his cattle at the auction in Bitterroot Springs shortly afterward, carrying a new brand."

"Rebranding? It sounds like more than one rustler is involved," Hardin replied.

"If you need assistance with either issue, Marshal, we're here to help. However, right now, I have lots of soldiers in training, and my officers need my confirmation for this group to graduate."

"That's fine. I should be on my way anyway, Colonel. It was a pleasure meeting you."

"Do come and visit sometime. We'll share a meal and some wine with my officers."

"Thank you, Colonel. A meal sounds wonderful."

Hardin was then escorted outside by a soldier, where he mounted Amos and quickly rode away.

7

After arriving in Bitterroot, Hardin took Amos to the livery before heading to the café for a quick bite. Waitress Lydia Travers brings him a glass of tea and places it on the table.

"I've been looking for you around town," Lydia says with a friendly smile.

"My job takes me out of town a lot," Hardin replied. "Today, just bring me the special?"

Lydia smiled at him. "Coming right up," she replied, then headed toward the kitchen. A few moments later, she returned with a plate of beans, potatoes, and slices of freshly baked bread. "The bread is still warm from the oven."

"Smells fresh. Did you make it?" Hardin inquired.

Lydia smiled and said, "Yes. I don't always cook, but I did today. Got to run, but you can tell me what you think."

As Hardin enjoyed his meal, he watched Lydia and Darci West serve the patrons with impressive speed. When he finished, he wiped his mouth with a towel as Glenn Barlow walked up to his table.

"Marshal, I see you're still hanging around our town. If you stay too long, it might just grow on you," Barlow said with a hearty laugh.

"I'll be here until I finish my work," Hardin replied. "It's a shame you can't find a sheriff for this town. Surely, a man will come along, but don't just hire anybody, Barlow."

"Yeah, I understand what you mean. We've had a few men apply who didn't meet our standards. Thankfully, someone knew them well enough to give us a heads up."

"That's good to hear," Hardin replied.

"Well, got some work to attend to, so I should get going," Barlow said.

"Yes, I've got plenty, myself," Hardin replied. He rose from his chair and waved at Lydia. As he placed money on the table, she made her way to him.

"Maybe I'll see you later, Marshal," Lydia said with a grin.

"Yeah, perhaps," he replied. "And the bread was perfect."

"Oh, thanks."

Someone called Lydia over to their table as Hardin put on his hat and stepped outside the café. Standing on the porch and looking over the town, he noticed two men in a wagon backing a load of lumber toward the mill about a quarter mile away. Curious, he wondered if they were part of the group of timber cutters that Cornelius Vance had cheated and started walking in their direction.

The water-powered sawmill emitted a sharp sound as the blade hit the log, a jarring noise that hurt Hardin's ears. He watched the operation for a moment as men unloaded logs onto a lumber skid while the sawyers cut them into boards and stacked the finished pieces neatly on another skid.

One of the men from the wagon spotted Hardin and headed his way. "Are you the Marshal Duncan that Caleb mentioned?" he asked.

"I am," Hardin replied. "U.S. Marshall Hardin."

"My name is Josiah Reed. I was hoping to catch you in town. I wanted to let you know that Vance still hasn't paid my men for their work," he said.

"I rode out to Vance's place and had a conversation with him," Hardin remarked. "I'm sorry that the rancher is reluctant to pay. He assured me he would meet with you to resolve the issue."

"That can only mean he has something up his sleeve," Josiah replied.

"What do you mean by that?" Hardin asked, raising an eyebrow.

"Marshal, Vance has all those cowboys working for him, and I hear some of them are gunfighters. My men can't go up against them—we wouldn't stand a chance. The problem is, these men are angry and may try to force Vance into paying them."

"No, they shouldn't confront him directly. Let the law take care of this."

"You're the only law we've seen in these parts for some time, Marshal, besides that no-good sheriff at Miles City. Even you can't face them alone?"

"Josiah, just give it a few more days. If Vance does anything other than pay you, find me. I'll see if the army will get involved."

"I hope he pays up, Marshal, because I might not be able to hold these men back. They lost a good three weeks of payroll on that deal."

Struggling to hear over the noise of the mill, Hardin moved a few steps away and gestured for Josiah to follow. "One more thing. Don't forget to consult a lawyer to have a contract drawn up. Get it signed by both the landowner and the mill. A contract would protect you if this happens again—it's like insurance."

"Yeah, I'll look into it," Josiah replied. "These men don't have a lot of money, so hopefully it fits into our budget."

"If there aren't any lawyers in town, there's bound to be one in Miles City," Hardin said.

Josiah's companion signaled he was ready to leave. "Marshal, I need to head out," he said. "I'll speak to a lawyer and keep you posted if Vance pulls anything."

Hardin watched the two men climb into their wagon and head through town as he walked toward the general store. An elderly woman tended to the goods on a shelf as he entered.

"Ma'am, could you point me to the gloves?" Hardin asked.

"They're on the back aisle, by the hardware," she replied.

"Thank you," He said and walked down the main aisle until he spotted the gloves neatly arranged on a shelf. As he slipped his right hand into one to try it on, he felt a light brush against his side. Turning, he met Lydia's bright smile. He almost didn't recognize her in her lovely pale lavender dress, its bodice and skirt adorned with intricate ruffles and lace. A matching lavender and white hat, with elegant lace, framed her blond hair and made her warm eyes sparkle.

"Hello, Marshal," Lydia said softly. "I guess all cowboys need a good pair of gloves. Oh, but wait—you're not a cowboy; you're a marshal." She offered him a playful smile."

"Fancy running into you here, Lydia, especially dressed so stylishly, though I understand why you'd come. A woman has to eat."

"That's right—my cooking is not limited to the café."

Nodding appreciatively, he said, "I'm sure that's true, ma'am."

"Marshal, I'm still waiting for that buggy ride."

A faint blush crept onto Hardin's face. "I... I thought you were just teasing or making casual conversation at the café," he admitted.

"I don't joke about such things," she replied.

"Look, you don't really know me—where I'm from or what I've been through," he said. "I'm sure there are other men around who'd be eager to make your acquaintance."

His words struck her deeply. Being rejected by a man wasn't typical for Lydia. Though thankful she had never worked in a brothel, her experiences in New Orleans and St.

Louis taught her the importance of finding the ideal man to settle down with. When she met Marshal Reuben Hardin, something about him just felt right. "I didn't mean to scare you away, Marshal. I only want to be friends," Lydia replied, hoping it would take their conversation in a different direction.

Hardin could sense that he had offended her. "Perhaps I was being hasty, but I know so little about you."

"We can get to know each other during a buggy ride and a picnic," Lydia suggested. "I'll bring what we need if you rent a buggy and a horse from the livery. I know a lovely spot near a beautiful creek, with plenty of shade, perfect for spreading out a blanket and just relaxing."

"Alright, when do you want to go?" Hardin asked.

"I think I can get away from the job in the morning. I'll ask Joe and let you know, Marshal."

"Tomorrow works for me, unless something unexpected comes up," Hardin said.

"Alright, I'll come by later and let you know," Lydia said as she turned and headed toward the door.

Hardin watched as the gorgeous woman stepped out of the general store, glancing back over her shoulder. As he lingered in the aisle, fixated on her, Charles Stewart, the owner and proprietor, leaned casually against the end cap. "She's a beauty, ain't she, mister?"

"Um, you mean..." Hardin replied, turning to him.

"Yeah, Lydia. The woman's a fine catch. I don't believe I've met you," Charles said, spotting the badge. "Do we have a new sheriff?"

"U.S. Territorial Marshal Reuben Hardin, he replied, introducing himself."

"I'm happy to meet you, Marshal," Charles replied. "Did you find everything you were looking for?"

"Yes, these gloves are perfect, sir."

"Alright, let's get you to the checkout, Marshal."

Hardin paid for his gloves and stepped outside, still toiling with meeting Lydia. Was he ready to let a woman into his life again? How long could it last with him riding out so often after outlaws and desperados? Only time would tell.

8

The alley lay shrouded in shadows between the buildings as Hardin and his deputy moved cautiously down the path. Witnesses had seen the suspect flee into the darkness after firing shots toward the saloon. Hardin gazed at the hazy path ahead, worried his deputy, Thaddeus Morrow, might catch the scent of whiskey as they moved forward. It didn't matter, though—he had to identify the shooter and bring them in.

The only light came from the soft glow of nearby houses and businesses, but he thought he spotted movement behind an old whiskey barrel.

Thaddeus whispered, "I think I see him, Sheriff, on the other side of the barrel."

Hardin called out, "You better come out with your hands up."

The man fired two shots that ricocheted off the building behind them before Hardin fired back—once, then again. The perpetrator stood for a moment, then slumped over the barrel, collapsing to the ground.

Thaddeus stepped forward first. "Sheriff, he's just a kid. That's the mayor's son. I should find his father." As Thaddeus hurried away, Hardin kneeled beside the youthful figure. He gazed through the darkness at the youngster's face—so young, lying there unmoving. Kyle Gittens was only fourteen—a detail that echoed through Hardin's mind from a recent conversation with his father.

Voices grew louder as the crowd began to gather behind Hardin.

Mayor Wayne Gittens looked down at his son, shaking his head in disbelief, then turned a fierce gaze toward Hardin. "*You* killed my boy!" He stepped closer, gripping Hardin's shirt in anguish. "Why, why, why?" His voice softened as he locked eyes with Hardin. "You've been drinking whiskey again—I smell it. Get your things out of the sheriff's office. You're fired!"

As Hardin walked back toward the office, still shaken from what he had done, he could hear Gittens shouting, "Leave this town, Hardin. You're not welcome here anymore!"

But suddenly, another sound grew loud in his ears, pulling Hardin from his reflections. Still rattled, he slowly opened his eyes, realizing he had been dreaming. As the remnants of the nightmare lingered in his mind, someone knocked insistently on the door, fully waking him. Forcing himself to roll over, he sat on the edge of the bed.

"I'm coming," Hardin called out. "Just give me a minute."

He reached for his pants and slipped them on, fastening them as he made his way to the door.

"Marshal, you don't know me, but I need your help. I work for a cattle ranch just outside Miles City—the Moore Ranch. We knew we'd had cattle stolen several times and couldn't figure out who was behind it. I was on watch last night when five men struck again. I couldn't take them on alone, so I followed them to a spot between here and Miles City. I heard there was a marshal in Bitterroot Springs, so I rode here to find you. I'm sorry for waking you so early, but I really need your help."

As Hardin rubbed his eyes and looked at the man again, he asked, "What's your name?"

"Colt Jackson."

Hardin grabbed his shirt and slid his arm into a sleeve. "And who did you say you worked for?"

"James Moore, Marshal."

"Would that happen to be James Alexander Moore?" Hardin asked.

"Yeah, I've heard him called that. Do you know him?"

"Oh, yes. We worked together several years back on the Pony Express."

"So, will you help us, Marshal?"

"Sure, if you don't mind letting me finish getting dressed, "Hardin replied. "Meet me at the café across the street—I need to grab a quick bite before we head out," he added, sensing a long day ahead.

"I'll be there," Colt responded and left the room.

In just a few moments, Hardin had dressed, put on his boots, cinched his gun belt, and grabbed his saddlebags and rifle before stepping out of the hotel room. He crossed the street and entered the café, hoping to see Lydia, only to remember that she had asked for the morning off. She had not sent word, but they were planning to go on a buggy ride and picnic in a few hours—he figured she'd understand that work called. Taking a seat at a table across from Colt Jackson, he asked, "Have you ordered?"

"No. I wasn't sure how much of a hurry you were in to leave."

"They're quick with breakfast. Colt, you should eat something—it might be a long day."

"Marshal, I don't get paid until Saturday."

"Order whatever you'd like—I'll take care of it. You can buy mine sometime in the future."

Darci West approached the table. "What can I get for you gents?"

"Get this man whatever he wants and put it on my ticket," Hardin instructed.

Colt ordered biscuits and gravy with coffee, while Hardin chose his usual: two eggs over easy, bacon, and two biscuits—one of which he always carried to eat with his coffee.

As Darci walked away, Colt looked at Hardin. "I never got your name, Marshal."

"Marshal Reuben Hardin, but just call me Hardin. That's what everyone else calls me."

"Alright."

"Colt, how long has James been running cattle?" Hardin asked.

"Well, he made me foreman two years ago, but I've been working at the ranch for five years. Mr. Moore had cattle before I came, so I can't really say for certain."

"James and I lost touch after they shut down the Pony Express."

"Marshall, they bring mail to Miles City on the freighters now," Colt said. "I believe a steamboat brings it close enough for them to pick it up."

"You're right, Colt. I spoke with a freighter, and he said he picks up supplies at Glendive Cantonment from a steamboat."

Darcy soon brought their breakfast and set it on the table. In a while, they finished eating, and Hardin headed to the livery to get his horse. He followed Colt as they rode away from Bitterroot.

"How many cows have gone missing from Moore's ranch in total?" Hardin asked as they rode alongside each other.

"Last month, we lost thirty-five, Marshal. So far this month, twenty, and it's early."

"Maybe we can shut this down before it gets worse," Hardin said. "Can you handle that hog leg you've got strapped on?"

"I might not win a gunfight, but I can hit what I aim at," Colt replied. "That's what matters."

After about seven miles of riding, Colt slowed his horse. "We're getting close to where we need to turn."

"You're looking for a marker," Hardin deduced.

"Just an old oak that's been struck by lightning," Colt replied. "How can you tell that in the dark?"

"Well, I've been through this way before. When I get to the road, I recognize my surroundings." Colt looked ahead and declared, "That's where we need to go."

Through the woods, the young foreman led them down a deer trail—the horse tracks in the dirt suggested that other riders had used it.

"There've been a few horses besides yours through this way," Hardin noted.

"They probably took the trail just like I did to shorten their ride," Colt replied.

A few hundred yards away, Colt stopped. "We should tie our horses here and continue on foot," he whispered.

They dismounted and secured their horses to nearby trees and a grassy knoll. Colt then led the way through the woods as Hardin drew his gun from its holster.

"It's just up ahead," Colt explained.

Peering from behind some trees, they could see smoke rising from a fire, but there were no cattle, horses, or riders in sight.

"I think they've left, Marshal," Colt determined.

Hardin stepped around the young ranch foreman and approached the camp. Only a few coals remained in the fire, with the branding iron lying beside it. "This is where they re-branded the cattle," he remarked, picking up the iron by its handle. "It's clear what they're doing—they're taking Moore's cattle, already branded with an 'M,' and adding their own."

"No wonder they're hitting us so hard," Colt replied.

Hardin tossed the branding iron aside. "Do you know of any ranches using the double M?"

"I don't know any. Must be a new outfit, Marshal."

"The stockyard should have some information," Hardin said.

"The only one nearby is in Miles City," Colt replied. "Ranchers sell their cattle there, and then they're herded to the steamboat for shipment to Chicago."

"Why don't they use the train?" Hardin asked.

"Mr. Moore says they will once they get enough cooler cars. I can't explain it beyond that," Colt replied.

"I believe they call them open-air stock cars or boxcars with grated doors for ventilation," Hardin said. "They already have them in Kansas and are likely producing more." He gazed around the camp and said, "We should leave before these men return."

"Yes, we'd better," Colt agreed.

As they reached their horses, Colt turned to Hardin. "What will you do, Marshal?"

"Well, now that I know where their base camp is, I can set up nearby and keep an eye on them. But first, I'm going to ride to the stock-yards to find out who's running the Double M brand."

"Then I need to find Mr. Moore and let him know where I've been. He's probably fit to be tied," Colt said.

"Yeah, right. I'll ride with you to Miles City."

They mounted their horses and rode away from the branding grounds.

9

As Colt continued toward James Moore's ranch, Hardin made his way to the stockyard office. After dismounting and stepping inside, he found the place empty, so he slipped out the back door, where a large lot held cattle waiting for cowboys to herd them to the steamboat. Two men stood on the wooden fence, directing the cattle into a chute, while another man at the far end jotted down something on a notepad.

Hardin soon approached the man with the notepad. "Could one of you help me look up some brands?" he asked.

The man with the pencil stopped and looked him over. "Who are you?"

"I'm Marshal Reuben Hardin," he said.

"Hello, Marshal. I'm Rufus Hale. I've heard there's a new Marshal in the area. You'll have to wait just a moment while we check this batch of cattle for shipping."

"I can wait," Hardin replied.

Thirty minutes passed, and they finished their checks. Hale called out to his men, "I'm going to help this man for a minute. Get the next batch ready while I'm gone."

Hale led Marshal Hardin into his office and went straight to a file cabinet. After a quick search, he found what he needed and laid it on the counter in front of Hardin. "Here's what I have, Marshal."

"I'm looking for the double M brand," Hardin said.

"Got it right here—it belongs to a man named Matt Moran," Hale replied.

"Moran. Do you know him?" Hardin asked.

"Marshal, I've only seen him around. Don't know much about him; he showed up here about a month ago, and I've noticed him leaving the sheriff's office a couple of times," he explained.

"Hmm. May I take a look at the others?"

"Sure, feel free to check them out as much as you want. Just leave them on the counter when you finish—I have to get back to the stock," Hale said.

"Of course, go ahead," Hardin replied.

There were a total of seven top ranches based at Miles City. After looking over them all, he headed outside toward his horse as a buckboard pulled up beside him.

"I can't believe it. Reuben Hardin in Montana! What brings you north?" the man asked.

Shaking his head in disbelief, Hardin replied, "James Moore. Considering the risks you took riding for the Express, I expected you'd be dead by now."

"I ought to be," Moore responded with a laugh. "But at least I'm not foolhardy enough to take on a U.S. Marshal's job."

"I suppose I've gotten better at taking on risks as I've gotten older," Hardin admitted.

The smile faded from Moore's face. "It doesn't get much riskier than going after cattle thieves. Colt filled me in on all of that. I just wish he had woken me up and warned me what he was up to—I nearly offered his foreman position to someone else."

"No one's caught them yet," Hardin pointed out.

"Would you like a couple of men to go along and help?" Moore offered.

Hardin looked down at the ground, considering Moore's generosity. "I'm concerned they might kill the rustlers, and I need them alive to face charges."

"Make your intentions clear to them, Reuben. I want to see them charged, as well. I have two men you can trust, and I'll loan them to you."

"Alright, send them to the café, but tell them not to mention this to anyone," Hardin instructed.

Moore furrowed his brows. "You don't know who they are yet."

"That's right, and I want to catch them red-handed," Hardin stated.

"I'll send them as soon as I get this feed to the ranch. It's really great to see you, Reuben," Moore said, snapping the reins to urge the team forward.

Two men on horses rode into Miles City and reined up at the café.

"I don't see why Moore wants us to fight with cattle thieves," Choro remarked.

"Because we can't afford to lose any more cattle," Buck Higgins responded as he dismounted. "The marshal will handle most of it anyway."

Choro gave him a stern look. "Moore, tell me, 'do what he say.'"

"We will, but we're not looking to kill anyone," Higgins replied.

They entered the café and spotted a tough-looking man with a badge sitting alone at a table and approached him. "You must be the marshal," Higgins said.

"Are you Moore's men?" Hardin asked.

"Yes, sir. I'm Buck Higgins, and this is Choro. We're here to help you."

"Alright, let's head that way. If you need any supplies, grab them before we leave. We'll camp a few hundred yards from them until we hear the cattle bellowing." Hardin stood up, put on his hat, and led them out the door.

"I'm going to pick up some chewing tobacco from the general store," Higgins said.

"You'd better grab some beans and bacon for your meals. I don't have enough food for all of us."

Higgins nodded as he mounted his horse and rode up the street.

While waiting for Higgins beside their horses, Hardin glanced at Choro, noting the intricate beadwork on his leather attire. "What's your name again?" he asked.

"Choro," he replied, speaking with a Native American accent.

"What tribe do you belong to?" Hardin continued.

"The Hopi Nation—a small band," Choro answered.

"Are you also a cowhand working for James Moore?"

"Yes, and I track when he asks."

"I'm pleased to meet you," Hardin said.

Choro nodded as he glanced down the road and saw Higgins mounting his horse at the general store. "Higs coming now," he said.

The two men followed Hardin to a camping spot he had chosen, situated about a quarter mile from the branding site and two hundred yards from the trail. "We'll set up camp here," he said. "There's a creek nearby, and we're close enough to hear the cattle when they bring them in for branding."

"You know it might be a long wait, Marshal, before those men show up?" Higgins remarked.

"Yeah, I know," Hardin replied. "So, we'll give it a couple of days. I want to get to the bottom of this cattle rustling business, so make yourselves comfortable."

10

Choro gently shook Marshal Hardin, who lay tucked in his bedroll. "I hear the cows, Marshal. Do you want me to wake Higs?" he asked.

"No, let him sleep, Choro. We can't do anything until daylight. I'll head out for a quick look, but I'll be back soon."

After Hardin got himself awake, he followed the same path as before, the sounds of the cattle growing louder with each step. As he neared the opening where they carried out their rebranding, he spotted a small herd and a fire burning through the trees.

Carefully, he stepped out from the woods, closer to the herd. "Easy now," he whispered to one of the steers. Under the moon's gentle glow, the faint letters 'MI' on the cow's hip caught his eye, a brand he knew would soon be changed to 'MM'.

Turning back toward the woods, Hardin retraced his steps and soon emerged from the trees near the camp, where Choro waited for him. "Yes, they're definitely changing brands," Hardin said. "I suspect they'll rest for a while before getting to work. Choro, you should get some rest—I'll keep watch."

"No, I stay up with you. Only a few hours will be sunshine," Choro insisted.

"Suit yourself. I'm going to sit by the fire and read my Bible," Hardin replied. While Choro settled back against his saddle, Hardin tended to the fire.

As early dawn broke, Choro woke Buck Higgins, and Hardin began boiling a pot of coffee.

Higgins stirred from his blanket, groaning softly as he stretched his stiff limbs. "Feels awful early," he mumbled, squinting at the faint dawn.

"It is," Hardin said, poking at the campfire's embers. "But those boys'll start branding soon, and we need to be ready."

Higgins sat up, rubbing his eyes. "The rustlers came already?"

"Yes, several hours ago."

"Well, thanks for letting me catch a bit more shut-eye," Higgins said, his yawn breaking the morning quiet.

"Coffee will be ready in just a moment," Hardin said. "Drink it quickly so we can bring this bunch in."

Higgins nodded, a faint grin tugging at his lips. "Sounds good to me. Maybe we'll get to sleep in a bed tonight. Even the bunkhouse beats this hard ground."

One cowboy crouched by the fire, stoking the flames and pushing the branding iron into the coals. Nearby, another lassoed a steer and pulled it toward the heat. An older cowboy roped the next steer, guiding it to the fire where they quickly burned the brand into its hide.

"Boone, watch you don't leave any trace of the old brand," Dean Dunmore said.

Boone Rogers gave a quick nod, wiping sweat from his brow. "Doing my best, Dean."

"It's gotta pass as a double M," Dean added. "If any of them looks off, they'll question the whole lot."

"I got it, Dean," Boone replied with irritation in his voice.

Dean glanced up as his two ropers rode back to the fire empty-handed. "Where are your steers, Matt? Earl?" he asked, his voice tinged with anger.

Matt's face contorted with unease. Before Dean could press him further, a man he didn't recognize walked from behind the pair. Dean's hand naturally moved to his holster, drawing his revolver as another stranger emerged from behind their horses.

Then a sharp, authoritative voice barked from behind him, "Hold it right there. Drop your gun!"

Dean spun around, his heart pounding, and saw his other man, Wallace Rogers, standing with his hands raised high, escorted by a rugged-faced man with a badge and a gun.

"Sorry, Dean," Wallace muttered, his voice laden with regret. "He came out of the woods like a ghost. Didn't even have a chance to draw."

"You two on the horses, dismount and get on the ground," Hardin ordered. "The rest of you, hold it where you are."

Dean watched Hardin as he walked in front of them. "Don't worry, men—I'll figure a way out of this," he murmured.

Hardin snapped the hammer back on his revolver, leveling it at Dean's chest. "So, how do you figure to wiggle out of this when we caught you red-handed, rebranding those steers? I'm taking you in for cattle rustling."

"You've got it wrong, Marshal," Matt Staap, the grizzled older man, declared firmly. "We bought those cows outright."

Buck Higgins sneered. "That's a lie, and we all know it. You've been stealing Mr. Moore's cattle for months."

"Check the brands," Dean fired back. "Not one of those cows carries Moore's mark."

"Choro, tie their hands in front of them so they can mount their horses," Hardin instructed.

Boone turned to Dean, uncertainty flashing in his eyes. "Dean, are you sure you can get us out of this?"

"Don't worry, Boone. I know the sheriff," Dean replied confidently.

"Sheriff won't help you out of this," Choro remarked, a note of assurance in his tone.

Once Choro finished tying their hands, Higgins brought their horses over and helped them mount up. Choro secured them to the saddle horns and gathered their reins. When he had the last one tied, he called out, "Marshal, they ready."

"Let's get them to jail," Hardin replied.

Marshal Hardin led the way along the path, with the rustler's horses strung together with a rope. Choro and Higgins followed closely behind, keeping watch until they reached town. As they came into Miles City with the rustlers, a growing crowd gathered to witness the commotion.

Sheriff Shepard quickly stepped out of his office when he heard the disturbance. "Hardin, what's all this?" he asked.

"Cattle rustlers," Hardin explained. "Caught them in the act, changing brands."

"Marshal, you should have given me a heads-up before bringing them here," Shepard declared, displeasure in his voice.

"Sheriff, I can't warn you every time I come across a crime. Their branding grounds were out of your jurisdiction."

"Still, I like a heads up on such things," Shepard replied.

Hardin gave him a stern look. "Do you have room in your jail for them?"

Shepard observed the rustlers, his jaw tight. He knew if he didn't take them, Hardin would likely send them to the army's jail—a grim place, by all accounts, unfit for any man. "Yeah, I'll make room. Bring 'em in."

Ranch owner Nathaniel Boone fell into step beside Buck Higgins as they walked. "Buck, whose cattle did they steal?" he asked.

"This lot is from Ike McInnes' ranch," Higgins answered, glancing at the bound men. "You lose any cattle, Mr. Boone?"

"Not yet. We've been watching our herd like hawks," Nathaniel replied. "What about your boss?"

"Rustlers hit us twice. Reckon we're down about fifty head," Higgins said.

"This has to stop," Nathaniel remarked firmly.

"That Marshal means business," Higgins said. "He's really trying to clean things up."

"Good. I need a word with him," Nathaniel said, but could see that Hardin and the Sheriff were busy with the prisoners.

The five thieves walked into the jail, and Sheriff Shepard locked them in the cells as curious townsfolk peered through the door.

"Hey, Sheriff, we need water in here!" Dean Dunmore bellowed, gripping the bars.

"Settle down, Dunmore," Shepard shot back, shutting the hallway door with a heavy thud.

Hardin stood near Shepard's desk, contemplating how the sheriff seemed to be acquainted with Dunmore. "Sheriff, do you have any circulars on any of these?"

Shepard rubbed his chin, frowning. "I'll check, but I don't believe I do. Look, Hardin, we need to work together to catch the criminals. It'd make my job easier."

Hardin bit back a response, reminding himself that he wasn't there to make anyone's job easier; he would just do his work. "I'll do what I can, Sheriff, but I can't always tip you off in advance. Now, I expect you to keep these men locked up until the judge sees them or transfers them to another jail."

"Yeah, alright. You got them here, Hardin. Now what happens?" Shepard asked, crossing his arms.

Hardin turned toward the door. "They have to go before the judge. I'll send word to him right away."

Shepard leaned back, his chair creaking. "Fair warning, Marshal Hardin—even if you send word to Judge Quinn today, it might be two weeks before he sets a date for them. Shelton Quinn ain't one to rush."

"Those men won't mind keeping you company. The judge'll likely sentence them to hang, so they should enjoy the extra time they have," Hardin said.

Shepard's gaze dropped to the scuffed floor. "You're probably right. Doesn't mean I have to like it."

"Neither do I," Hardin admitted, his tone softer but firm. "But they've got to answer for their crimes, Sheriff."

"I know that."

"Alright, Sheriff, I'm going to grab something to eat. I'll let you know when I hear from Judge Quinn."

"Yeah, do that. Now, get out of here," Shepard growled.

Nathaniel lingered outside the jail, waiting for Hardin to step outside. "Marshal, I need to talk with you."

"What's on your mind?" Hardin asked, pausing to meet his gaze.

"I saw three of those rustlers huddled in the alley by the saloon a week ago," Nathaniel said. "I reckon they were plotting the cattle you found them with."

Hardin's eyes narrowed. "Did you overhear them scheming?"

"No, I was too far away," Nathaniel admitted. "But can't the judge use what I just told you against them?"

Hardin shook his head. "I'm afraid that won't hold up in court. However, with what we saw them involved with today, it should be enough to lock them away for a good long while."

Nathaniel nodded slowly. "I hear you. Well, thanks for putting a stop to them, Marshal."

"Just doing my job," Hardin replied.

Choro and Higgins waited beside the horses as Hardin came to them. "Men, thanks for your help in bringing in those men," he said.

"No, thank you, Marshal," Higgins declared. "Mr. Moore'll want to thank you, too."

"Let's just hope they're the only bunch rustling cattle," Hardin replied.

"What about their horses?" Choro asked, patting one of them.

Hardin gestured to the end of town. "Take 'em to the livery. Tell them the town and sheriff will cover the board."

Higgins let out a dry chuckle. "That should make the mayor happy."

Hardin cracked a smile. "After you finish, meet me at the café. Lunch is on me."

"Sounds great," Higgins said, swinging into his saddle and turning toward the livery stable.

11

Dean Dunmore rattled the jail cell door. "You can let us out now, Shepard—that Marshal is gone."

Shepard stepped into the cell hallway. "Can't do that."

"Why not?" Dean pressed.

"You knuckleheads put yourselves in this mess, and now you expect me to fix things for you."

"Sheriff, that judge will hang us," Matt Staap said.

"Maybe he should for your stupidity," Shepard replied.

"Shepard, you're in this as much as we are," Dean declared. "If you don't get us out, I'm sure the judge would love to know your involvement."

"We'll just see about that," Shepard retorted. "What you don't realize is that Shelton Quinn is my brother–in–law, and we are fishing buddies. You should've posted a lookout, Dean. How could you overlook that?"

"Are you just gonna leave us in here?" Dean shouted.

"Tomorrow," Shepard replied coolly. "You need to spend a night in jail to think about your stupidity."

"Then at least get us some water," Dean said, his tone softening. "And maybe a little coffee."

"I'll bring you water," Shepard replied. "You'll get your supper around six, and I'll let you out in the morning after breakfast."

"This will cost you, Sheriff," Dean warned.

"Dean, it's already costing me plenty." Shepard closed the door.

Dean shook the jail door loudly. "Don't forget about our water!"

All day, Hardin couldn't shake thoughts of Lydia from his mind. After finishing lunch with the other men, he mounted Amos and rode toward Bitterroot Springs. He expected Lydia to be at work when he arrived, but felt it was important to talk to her and explain why he had missed their outing a few days before. If she were like the other women he had known, she would think a picnic outweighed the urgency of catching criminals. Perhaps she would understand and give him a chance to make amends.

After camping for a few hours in the early evening, he quickly gathered his belongings and pressed toward Bitterroot Springs. The moon lit the trail as he rode, watching for a few tricky spots. Just past noon, he arrived in town and reined in at the livery stable just as Ezra Tate stepped outside.

"Hello, Marshal," Ezra said, his eyes scanning Hardin's horse. "I didn't expect to see you back in Bitterroot so soon."

"I wrapped things up early," Hardin replied, glancing at him as Ezra looked across the street.

"Marshal, have you met Silas Granger?" Ezra asked, turning toward the approaching fur trader.

Hardin watched as Silas approached. "Yes, we've met before."

Silas smiled warmly as he reached them. "How have you been, my friend?"

"Dandy enough," Ezra responded. "Are you having any luck trapping these days?"

Silas replied with a grin, "Catching as many as I can." He peered around Ezra and noticed Hardin. "Well, Marshal, I see the bears haven't eaten you."

"Not yet," Hardin said.

Silas chuckled. "I bet you haven't even spotted one."

"You guessed right," Hardin admitted.

"Don't fret about the bears for now," Silas continued. "They're down in the valley, feasting on trout from the creeks and rivers. They'll catch up to you soon enough—I just hope they've had their fill by the time you pass through."

Hardin's eyes widened at the remark.

Silas laughed heartily, prompting the other two men to join in his amusement.

"Silas, what brings you out of the forest?" Hardin asked, intrigued to see if the old-timer had any news to share.

Silas chewed on his tobacco wad and spat on the ground, locking eyes with the Marshal. "I might have something for you."

"Oh, really?" Hardin replied, leaning in with interest.

"I once told you to keep an eye on Sheriff Shepard."

"Yes, you did, Silas."

"Now, this is just hearsay—I can't confirm it," the trapper cautioned.

"Go on," urged Hardin, his curiosity piqued.

"Marshall, I picked up supplies at Trader Jim's last week, right after I met you on the trail. An old trapper named Carrigan was there—that's all I know him by. Anyway, I overheard him telling some other men that Sheriff Shepard is the leader of one of those rustler gangs. He claimed he heard them in an alleyway in Miles City, making plans."

Hardin could hardly believe what Silas was saying. Sheriff Shepard had recently created space in his jail by releasing a couple of drunks early to accommodate the prisoners he had brought in.

"You're shaking your head, Marshal," Silas remarked. "Don't you believe me?"

"Yesterday, Sheriff Shepard took five rustlers into his jail for me. It's hard for me to see how he could be involved in cattle theft."

"Appearances, Marshal," Silas replied. "Shepard can't afford to let you know what he's up to. Besides, those you arrested may not even be his men."

Hardin shrugged his shoulders. "But to what end? If he gets caught in this, he knows I'll arrest him and he'll lose his badge."

Silas regarded him with a grin. "Marshal, I think once Shepard has enough money in his pocket, he'll tuck tail and run. Lawmen can be the worst kind of criminals; they know how to conceal their offenses."

"Marshal, Silas might have a point," Ezra added. "I've seen a lot of men coming in and out of the sheriff's office. Most of them aren't from around here."

"There you have it," Silas said, nodding in agreement.

"That's still no proof that Sheriff Shepard is involved in cattle rustling," Hardin stated.

"No, but it's starting to add up," Silas replied, noticing Ezra heading back inside. "Marshal, let me treat you to dinner at the café. I'll buy Ezra's too, if he'll stop working long enough."

"I appreciate the offer, Silas, but I need to see someone first. You might catch me there—the person I want to talk to works at the café."

"Well, that settles it then. You have to let me buy your supper," the trapper insisted.

"You two go ahead. I may not make it there for a while."

Silas shook his head. "You're going to miss out. Ezra and I are great company."

Hardin turned and walked toward the stables to put away his horse. "I'm sorry to miss it," he said.

Upon reaching the hotel, Hardin requested a bath. Knowing it would take some time to heat the water, he made his way upstairs to his room.

Lying back on the bed, he closed his eyes. His thoughts drifted to Hayes City and the night he shot Kyle Gittens. The kid had his whole life ahead of him, and in a moment, he had taken it all away. *God, will you ever forgive me for shooting that boy?* Tears welled in his eyes as he covered his face with his hands. *Why didn't Thaddeus just run me in?*

Lately, he had struggled to find sleep, haunted by the nightmares that forced him back to relive his handiwork with a gun.

A knock sounded on the door. "Yeah, I'm here."

From the other side, a voice announced, "Your bath is ready, sir."

Hardin opened the door to find an older man of Chinese descent smiling at him. "I'll be down in a moment."

He closed the door, quickly gathered a set of clean clothes, and made his way downstairs.

The Lonesome Pine Cafe buzzed with a lively crowd. Lydia scanned the room as she carried several hot meals to a table.

"Ma'am, when you have a moment," Sarah Holt said, "I could use a towel to wipe off my dress."

"And I need more tea," chimed in Gideon Holt, Sarah's husband and owner of Holt Bank.

"Give me one moment," Lydia replied. As she turned toward the kitchen, the main door swung open and Marshal Hardin stepped inside. *Great,* she thought.

As Hardin settled in at the only available table, Lydia returned to the kitchen for another round of plates. He scanned the room and soon spotted Lydia emerging with food, pausing briefly to exchange a few words with Darcy West. Darcy caught his eye and smiled.

After several long minutes, Darcy approached his table. "Hello, Marshal. I've heard quite a bit about you."

"All good, I hope," his voice laced with curiosity.

"That's a matter of opinion. What can I get for you today, Marshal?" Darcy asked.

"It looks like vegetable soup is on the menu. I'll take a bowl and whatever bread you have."

"Will cornbread do?"

"Certainly. Could you please let Lydia know that I'd like to speak with her?"

"I'll pass the message along, but I can't guarantee she'll come," Darcy replied.

"I understand."

"I assume you want tea to go with your meal?"

"Yes, please."

Darcy stopped by another table before making her way to the kitchen. Moments later, she returned to Hardin's table with his meal. "I spoke to Lydia, but she said she doesn't have time to talk tonight. Marshal, she's quite upset with you about something. You two will need to sort it out. Now isn't the right time for a conversation."

"Well, I appreciate you trying," Hardin replied. "Maybe I can catch up with Lydia tomorrow. Do you know where she lives?"

"She lives at Faye Rogers' boarding house, at the end of town."

"Thank you, Darcy."

"Of course." Darcy then turned her attention to another table.

After finishing his meal, Hardin rose to his feet. He watched Lydia for a moment, then turned and walked out of the café, heading back to the hotel.

12

The night brought heavy showers with thunder and lightning, making it difficult for Hardin to sleep. He could hear the rain pounding against the window and hitting something metal outside. The clouds made the morning darker than usual, yet Hardin sensed the dawn was near.

He got out of bed, washed his face. *Perhaps today, Lydia might feel like talking.* He quickly dressed, strapped on his weapon, and headed out of his room toward the café. As he expected, it was already bustling with activity.

Darcy West spotted Hardin and eagerly approached him. "Coffee, Marshal? The usual for breakfast, I assume?" she asked.

"That will be fine," Hardin answered.

A moment later, the waitress set a cup of black coffee in front of him. "Just a minute, and I'll bring out your breakfast."

"Is Lydia working this morning?" he asked.

"Lydia comes in before noon today, Marshal."

"Thank you."

Darcy returned shortly with his breakfast and a copy of the Bitterroot Chronicles. "I thought you might enjoy this while you eat." She placed it on the table.

"Thank you. I seldom have time to read it," Hardin replied.

"I figured as much. Enjoy your breakfast." She smiled warmly before moving on to attend to another table.

After finishing his breakfast, Hardin picked up the newspaper and noticed an article by Sarah Harlan—the headline read, 'More Trouble Between Timbercutters and Rancher Cornelius Vance.'

He murmured to himself, "That woman just stirs up hostility between those two parties. I'll need to have another conversation with her."

Taking a sip of his coffee, he glanced out the window and saw an elderly cowboy in a buckboard pulling up in front of the café. The man jumped from his seat and rushed through the door. After briefly scanning the room, he headed straight for Hardin's table.

"Marshal, you might have a shootout on your hands," he warned. "Well, I'll just say, I'm sure it's coming."

"Have a seat," Hardin replied. "You'll need to give me more than that."

Gasping for breath, the man pulled out a chair and sat down. "You see, I worked for Cornelius Vance."

"What's your name, and what do you mean by 'worked for him'?" Hardin asked.

"The name's Elijah Stone, and I've quit Vance. I *was* running fence line and doing other odd jobs no one else would do," he said. "I can't work for that man anymore. He's lost his mind."

Hardin's brow furrowed as he examined the old man. "What happened? Tell me everything."

" and almost all of his cowboys—plus those two gunhands he hired—are heading to the timber cutter's camp. There's going to be a fight. One of those cutters was at the saloon last night, badmouthing Vance for not paying them for their work.

"Go on," Hardin urged, leaning in to listen more closely.

"One of Cornelius Vance's cowboys came in this morning to see him, reporting that folks in the saloon were calling Vance a two-bit thief. Vance stood up from behind his desk, angry, and pointed to his gunmen, Gus Simmons, and the one you shot, Wesley Durant. He ordered them to gather the men and leave only two behind to watch the cattle. He said he was gonna handle the timber cutters once and for all. In about thirty minutes, they were on their horses, riding out."

Hardin took one last sip of his lukewarm coffee and rose to leave.

"What cha gonna do, Marshal?" Elijah asked.

"I'm going to do my best to stop them before anyone gets hurt," Hardin replied, making his way out the door.

Elijah Stone followed him outside. "Marshal, get in. I'll take you to the livery where you can get your horse."

"Thanks," Hardin replied and climbed into the wagon.

As the wagon rolled up to the livery and halted, Elijah added, "Marshal, I know you're goin' out there, but you can't stop all of them on your own. I want to help out—just try to stall them for a bit?

Hardin leaped down from the wagon and faced him. "Innocent men are bound to get hurt in this quarrel. I advise you to stay out of it."

Elijah locked eyes with him. "Can't do it. The folks around here rely on those timber cutters. Vance has to be stopped, and if you can't do it, I know men who will."

Hardin took a deep breath as he watched Elijah drive away. He had given the man a warning—there was nothing more he could do. In just a few minutes, he saddled Amos and set off toward the timber camp.

Cornelius Vance's men had positioned themselves on the far side of the road leading to the camp. Vance knew that women and children were present at the camp, and any violence against them would draw harsh criticism from the townsfolk. By drawing attention to the road, he aimed to protect the innocent.

Vance shouted across the road, "Josiah Reed, come out and talk. We need to settle this right now. No one will shoot."

"I hear you, Vance," Josiah responded. "*You* can settle it by paying what you owe."

"I never agreed to pay you anything," Vance retorted.

"Of course you did!" Josiah shouted angrily.

As Hardin rode closer, he overheard the tense conversation. Vance's men lined the side of the road, their eyes fixed on him.

Spotting Hardin's horse, Vance stepped boldly into the road. "What are you doing here, Marshal?" he called out as the lawman rode slowly past.

Hardin wheeled his horse around and reined him to a stop, locking eyes with Vance. "There will be no fight today. Take your men and go home."

Vance's face flushed with anger. "Our argument doesn't involve you, Marshal. Let us settle this today."

Hardin paused for a moment, glanced down at the rancher, then tightened his grip on the reins and pulled his horse back toward the camp. "If you go through with this, you'll have to get past me first."

"Now, Marshal!" Vance shouted, his face growing even redder with fury.

Hardin dismounted at the edge of the camp, where one of the men took Amos' reins and led him clear of the firing area.

From behind a building, Josiah Reed emerged. "Marshal, this fight is ours."

"Not if I can help it," Hardin responded.

The sudden rustle of leaves and breaking of branches drew their attention. They turned to see Elijah coming from the woods on a horse, accompanied by four more cowboys.

Elijah spotted the Marshal and called out, "I told you I had a plan. These men work for Amos Cutler, and they're here to help."

"I hope they won't have to," Hardin replied. "Get your horses back before the shooting starts."

Vance shouted again, "Josiah, bring your men out. Let's finish this fight."

Josiah turned to Hardin. "See, Marshal, the man only wants a fight."

Without a word, Hardin began walking down the road, his resolve apparent. "Vance, if you demand a fight, *I'll* give you one. These men are tree cutters and cowhands, not gunmen."

Vance glanced behind Hardin and saw the timbermen, along with those who had come with Elijah, lining up. Including Hardin, he counted fifteen men waiting, displaying their edge.

Turning to his gunmen, Vance asked, "I want one of you to take on Hardin?"

"I can," Wesley Durant answered.

"But your gun hand is injured," Vance responded. "How can you go up against him like that?"

"I've got another one," the gunman replied, raising his left arm. "I'll manage just fine."

Vance nodded. "I want both of you to get out there and take out the Marshal. With Hardin out of the way, I can deal with the rest."

Gus Simmons exchanged glances between Wesley Durant and Vance. "Now, we don't usually team up against a man. That doesn't help our reputation."

Vance's brow furrowed, and anger edged his voice. "There's an extra thousand dollars for each of you if you can take him down. But it has to be a joint effort! I want him eliminated today so he no longer poses a threat to my plans." Vance's idea of using both of them increased the chances that one of them might kill the marshal.

"We'll take care of him, Mr. Vance," Simmons replied confidently.

"Yeah, for good," Durant echoed.

The two men emerged from behind their cover and stepped onto the road, advancing toward the Marshal.

Hardin saw them making their approach. *So, this is how it's going to be?*

Simmons shot him a sneering glance. "Either of us can take you, Marshal. We might even give you a choice."

Durant leaned in toward Simmons and muttered, "Not if we want that extra thousand. Vance said we have to do this together."

"The Marshal doesn't know that, does he?" Simmons replied with a sly glint in his eye.

"Then how do you want to play it?" Durant asked quietly.

"When we're ready, you count down to three and we'll draw together," Simmons explained. "You'll naturally pull your gun first, because you're counting, and I'll follow. The plan will confuse him—he doesn't know which one of us is fastest."

"Alright," Durant replied with a sneering nod.

They took a position twenty paces from Hardin, spreading about six feet apart. Simmons pushed his hat back on his forehead to get a clearer view. Durant let out a huge sigh, wiped his lips, and rested his good hand above his gun.

Hardin studied the gunfighters as they prepared to draw their weapons. "I see you still can't use that hand," he said.

"In a minute, you'll see how good my other hand works, and we'll be even," Durant retorted with a wide grin, revealing some missing front teeth.

"We don't have to do this, gentlemen," Hardin said earnestly. "No one needs to die today. Just get on your horses and ride out. Your boss is headed to jail for failing to pay the timber folks and for stirring up trouble. So, I doubt he'll be around to pay you after today."

"We'll see about that, Marshal," Simmons replied, his tone tinged with defiance.

As Simmons' words faded into the air, an uneasy silence settled over the moment. Hardin stared into the faces of the gunmen, knowing that a man's eyes often reveal his true intentions before he makes a move.

Durant whispered something to his partner as Hardin sensed the tension building. Without hesitation, Durant reached for his gun; however, Hardin was quicker, landing a bullet squarely in his chest. As his shot found its target, the other gunman drew his weapon from his holster, but Hardin held his position. He turned toward Simmons and fired twice before he could react.

Hardin walked over to assess their condition. The two lay sprawled on their backs, gazing blankly at the sky. He bent down to close their eyes, as others gathered nearby.

A short distance away, Vance stood silently, staring at the two dead gunmen while Hardin approached him. "Vance, tell your men to drop their guns," he commanded.

Vance quickly tossed his weapon to the ground and raised his hands. "Give up your guns, men—they've got us," he said.

Shaken by what they had just witnessed, Vance's cowhands were hesitant to defy Marshal Hardin. One by one, they stepped out onto the road and dropped their weapons in the dirt. "We're just cowboys, Marshal, trying to make a living," one of them said. "Vance is the one who made us do it."

"You men should get on your horses and ride out," Hardin instructed.

"What about our weapons?" another cowboy inquired.

"You can pick them up tomorrow at the mayor's office."

One of the men led Vance's horse to him. With his hands tied, Hardin helped him onto his mount, and they rode toward the Miles City Sheriff's Office.

Persistent Nightmares

*A fresh start is just a chance to get yourself
into a new kind of trouble. —Unknown*

13

The days since Hardin's arrival seemed to have passed quickly, but this was not Kansas, and he hoped that one day things would change for him. He recognized most of the faces having breakfast at the Lonesome Pine Café, but he wondered if they'd ever be friends, considering that William Boyd might someday send him back home.

After finishing his breakfast, Hardin sat quietly, savoring his coffee and watching folks through the window. As he gazed across the street at the general store, his thoughts turned to his haunting dream—the one that constantly reminded him of the young man he had killed. He wondered if the boy's family still resented him for what he did that night in the alley, even though it was their fourteen-year-old who had shot at them first. The dream often returned, disrupting his sleep, a burden he would carry for the rest of his life.

Shaking free of the bleak images, Hardin noticed a striking woman in a maroon velvet dress walking on the boardwalk. She soon reached the café door, opened it, and stepped inside. After finding Hardin sitting alone, she approached his table with a warm smile.

Looking down at him, she noticed the badge. "Hello, Sheriff, I'm Dr. Victoria Hawkins. What's your name?"

"Hardin. I'm actually a U.S. Marshal," he replied.

"Oh, I didn't realize there was a difference," she said, her tone reflecting a hint of curiosity.

"That's alright. I cover a large area, while the sheriff oversees a specific township," Hardin explained. "Right now, Bitterroot Springs is without a sheriff."

She flashed him a bright smile. "Then I'll be sure to seek your help when I need it."

"I heard you mention that you're a doctor," Hardin said, tilting his head slightly.

"Yes," Victoria replied, a smile dancing on her lips. "I'm opening a clinic about a mile out of town on the road to Miles City. I purchased a large plantation–style house right off the road to serve as both my home and my clinic."

"That's great to hear. I might need a bullet removed someday," he said.

She furrowed her brow, concern etching her features. "Are you expecting someone to shoot you, Marshal?"

Hardin chuckled. "You never know in my line of work." A sardonic smile tugged at his expression.

"May I ask something else, Marshal? Does anyone in town have a buggy for sale? I also need a horse. I just arrived on the stage and hoped to find them nearby."

"You might want to check the livery stable at the end of town," Hardin suggested. "I believe Ezra Tate rents them out. He should be able to fix you up."

"Thank you," Victoria said. "I suppose I should find a table and order something." She turned and walked away.

A doctor, he mused, watching her settle at a table. I wonder what kind of trouble has led her to such an unruly place?

Hardin finished his coffee and stepped outside, hoping he could follow the directions given by Darci West to the boarding house where Lydia stayed. He waved to the townsfolk as he strolled along the boardwalk, turning at the cross street. Just a couple of hundred feet from the corner, he spotted a gray house with a white picket fence and a trellis adorned with vibrant red and pink roses. He made his way to the porch and knocked on the door. When it opened, an older woman in a pale blue dress stood before him, eyeing him with curiosity. "I'm looking for Lydia Travers. Does she live here?" Hardin asked politely.

The woman, suppressing a smile, replied, "She does. May I ask who's calling on her?"

"Marshal Reuben Hardin, ma'am," he responded with a nod.

"Oh, a marshal! I'm Faye Rogers, and this is my boarding house," she said warmly. "Why don't you come in and wait in the parlor? I'll get her."

Hardin stepped inside, and she directed him to the parlor before heading to Lydia's room. Moments later, Faye returned. "I believe she'll be here shortly."

He stood, holding his hat in both hands as he met her gaze. "Thank you very much." He watched as the older woman disappeared down the hall.

Several minutes passed before he noticed Lydia standing in the doorway. "You've been avoiding me," Hardin said, his tone laced with frustration and concern.

"You avoided me first," Lydia countered, her expression guarded.

"I'm sorry how things turned out—I didn't mean to leave you hanging like that."

"Then why didn't you come tell me what was going on, Hardin?" she asked sharply.

"It was very early, and I didn't know where you lived," he explained.

"What was it this time?" she asked. "Did someone have a cow stuck in the mud and need your help?"

"Rustlers."

"I suppose it doesn't matter," Lydia said, crossing her arms. "I've figured you out. You're a marshal, and you'll always be off chasing criminals."

"That sounds about right," Hardin admitted with a slight nod. "You can never tell when trouble will crop up."

She stood there, staring at him in silence.

"I was hoping I could make it up to you," Hardin said, breaking the quiet. "I could rent a buggy for that picnic if you'd like."

Lydia pursed her lips and replied, her voice devoid of emotion, "I'm just not ready yet."

Nervously, he reached up to comb through his mustache. "Then... could we at least be friends? I'm hoping you won't dodge me."

She glanced down at the floor before meeting his gaze. "I suppose I can manage that."

Hardin smiled. "Great! I guess I'll see you at the café, then." He put on his hat and walked toward the entrance, turning to look at her one last time before opening the door. "Goodbye, Lydia."

She stayed quiet, watching him as he shut the door behind him. "Grrr..." she muttered, her teeth clenched in frustration.

14

The piano at the saloon played a lively tune as Hardin walked away from the livery stables, his hands still scented with neatsfoot oil after an hour spent conditioning his saddle leather. He reached the hotel and climbed the stairs to his room, eager to clean his weapons.

With a new cleaning rod and some paper patches from the general store, he worked on them. The addition of a third firearm to his arsenal—a 1876 model Winchester Centennial Rifle he had sighted in earlier that day—meant more maintenance, but the twelve-round capacity .45-75 caliber marked a welcomed upgrade from his old Hawkins Rifle.

He washed his hands in the washbasin, then stepped into the hallway to empty it from an opened window. Though the evening was still young, he decided to turn in early for a change. He blew out the kerosene lamp, slid beneath the covers, and soon fell asleep.

An hour later, a noise at the door roused him. He sat up in bed and reached for his gun. "What do you want?" he called out.

"Marshal, this is Grover French," came a muffled voice from the other side. "They sent me after you. There's been a shooting at the saloon."

"Ugh, give me a moment," Hardin grumbled, swinging his legs over the side of the bed.

He slipped on his britches and buckled his belt. Walking to the door, he cracked it open, sensing urgency. "Tell me again what happened."

"A couple of cowboys got into a fight at the saloon," French explained. "One man shot the other and then rode off. I reckon they were both drunk. Mayor Barlow also witnessed the matter and asked me to fetch you while he and a few others carried the body to the undertaker."

"How many witnesses are still at the saloon?" Hardin asked.

"Most of 'em, I reckon. Like I told you, Marshal, the cowboy who did the shooting and the mayor are gone, along with those who carried out the dead cowboy—but they'll be back soon enough."

"Go ahead and tell them not to leave," Hardin instructed. "I need to question every one about what they saw."

French met the lawman's gaze. "Marshal, I can tell you what you need to know."

"I'll hear your testimony too, but I need more than you to confirm it," Hardin said.

"Alright, I'll head back and tell them now," French said.

As French walked from the door, Hardin finished dressing and strapped his gun belt around his waist. He walked over to the chest, dipped a ladle into the hotel's water pail for a quick drink, then turned and left his room.

As Hardin made his way down the stairs, he found a moment to mull over Williams Boyd's parting words from Kansas City: "You have to earn your way back to Kansas if you want to be a sheriff again." He didn't resent being a marshal, but he missed being part of a community and getting to know the folks. A town sheriff felt closer to the pulse of the people—at least until a misstep unraveled things, as it had for him at Hayes City, Kansas. Boyd had staked his own reputation to wrangle him a second chance from his superiors. He couldn't squander it; one more slip, and the sheriff's badge might stay forever out of reach.

Hardin pushed through the swinging doors of the Saddlehorn Saloon, while the remaining men waited for him, hunched over their drinks.

One fellow lurched forward, his steps unsteady. "Marshal, I... saw... it all," he slurred, the whiskey on his breath marked him as too intoxicated to serve as a reliable witness.

Turning to the crowd, Hardin raised his voice over the low murmur. "Men, I need witnesses sober enough to give me an accurate account of what happened."

A man at the bar lifted his hand. "I saw it all, Marshal—name's Tom Carson. The shooter is Zeke Kane. He and Levi McCray were bellied up to the bar, drinking whiskey. I couldn't hear what passed between 'em, but McCray shoved Kane away and went for his iron. Kane was faster—dropped him right there at the end of the bar. He stood over the boy a spell, staring down, then bolted out the door. We all heard his horse hightailing it out of town."

Hardin scanned the room. "Is that about what the rest of you saw?"

"It is," Mayor Glenn Barlow said, walking back through the doors. "We all saw it go down, Marshal. Of course, Levi was dead, so we helped haul McCray's body to the under-taker. One of the hands mentioned he's got a brother on a cattle drive—someone ought to send word."

Hardin let out a sigh, eyeing the cluster of cowboys. "If this goes to court, I'll need a few of you to stand up and testify."

"I will, Marshal," Mayor Barlow replied with a firm nod.

"Appreciate it," he said, then shifted toward the men still huddled at the bar. "Does anyone know where I can track down Zeke Kane?"

"He rides for Amos Cutler," a young cowboy spoke up from the end of the bar.

"You look a mite young to be in a place like this," Hardin said.

"Seventeen, Marshal," he replied, straightening a touch.

"What's your name?"

The young man paused, glancing at his boots, then met Hardin's gaze. "Tobias Redd."

"I reckon you're all pals with Zeke, then?"

"Nah, Marshal," Tobias replied. "Most folks know McCray punches for the Cutler ranch. Some of us trail herds out of northern Montana."

Hardin nodded, noting the way the kid wore his gun low—hoping it was more bark than bite. "Much obliged, Tobias. What's Levi's brother's name?"

"Jedediah McCray. Goes by Jed."

"Thanks."

"Marshal, do you need me to show you to the undertaker?" Mayor Barlow inquired.

"That would be much appreciated," Hardin replied.

"Follow me, then."

They crossed the darkened street to Eli Whitaker's place and roused the man from his bed. "Sorry to drag you up again, Eli," Barlow said. "The marshal wants a look at the body we dropped off earlier."

Eli rubbed his eyes and nodded. "I'll fetch a lantern." He struck a match, the flame flickering behind him, then led them through the darkened parlor. "This way."

As Barlow and Hardin stepped into the back room, the cool air carried a faint tang of pine and earth. The young man lay still on the table, his face pale under the lantern's glow, and a strange coldness gripped Hardin—the sight dredging up visions of young Kyle Gittens.

"He's just a pup," Eli murmured, shaking his head. "Too young for this."

Barlow glanced at Hardin, whose face was ashen, even in the dead of night. "Marshal, are you alright?"

Hardin turned to him, steadying his breath. "Um, yeah, I reckon I've got a description in my head now."

"Thank you, Eli," Mayor Barton said. "We'll let you get back to bed." Once outside, he turned to Hardin. "You've seen your share of young fellas die before, haven't you, Marshal?"

"Too many, and it doesn't get easier," Hardin replied.

"They are much too young for these cattle drives."

"Oh, I don't know, Barlow. I was sixteen when I went on my first cattle drive. Better to see them herding beeves than holding up banks."

"You're right about that. Well, Marshal, I'm turning in for the night," Barlow said. "Just holler if you need anything."

"I sure will."

With that, Barlow turned and walked up the street, while Hardin made his way toward his room. Maybe this time, he thought, he could sleep straight through the night.

15

After a reluctant start to the day, Hardin dragged himself out of bed, quickly ate a simple breakfast, saddled his horse, and set off north from Bitterroot Springs in search of Amos Cutler's ranch. According to the directions Barton gave him, the place lay about seven miles north of the Powder River.

The trail wound through a wide canyon, where a herd of antelope grazed contentedly on the sparse early-winter grass. As Hardin crested the canyon's rim and entered the open plains, he spotted six Nez Perce riders skirting the edge of a wooded stand—a sight that set his nerves on edge. He kept them in view for about a mile as he pressed on, until the group veered toward the mountains.

At last, he reached a weathered sign that marked the Cutler Ranch and turned onto the rutted lane toward the main house. A few hands working with horses near the barn eyed him with curiosity as he drew near.

One of the men straightened up and called out, "Mister, what brings you here?"

Hardin reined in his horse and turned to face him. "I'm looking for Zeke Kane."

"Zeke's out with the herd right now," the man said. "But he figured you might show up."

As he spoke, a slender man, maybe fifty—bearded and wearing a wide-brimmed western hat—hurried over from the porch. He wore a plaid shirt beneath a brown leather vest and denim britches. "What does he want, Gideon?"

"He's looking for Zeke, Mr. Cutler," Gideon replied.

Hardin turned to face the ranch owner. "Sir, Zeke was involved in a shooting last night. I'm here to bring him in."

"The way I hear it, Zeke only fired in self-defense," Cutler said.

"I've heard the same, but it's for the judge to decide whether Zeke must stand trial."

"Marshal, why bother with a trial if Zeke's innocent?" Cutler asked.

"I don't make the laws, Mr. Cutler." Hardin retorted, his tone steady. "But I'm confident that once the judge hears the testimonies, he will dismiss the case."

"Have you ever dealt with Judge Shelton Quinn?" Amos Cutler asked.

"No, I haven't."

"That's right, you're new in these parts," Cutler said. "Well, let me tell you, Shelton Quinn's the harshest judge I've ever known. He's railroaded more than one innocent man straight to prison."

"Look, Mr. Cutler," Hardin said firmly. "I've got to take him in. If you try to stop me, the law won't take kindly to it."

Frustration etched across Amos Cutler's face as he turned to Gideon Walsh. "Saddle up one of the boys' mounts and have him ride out to find Zeke. Don't say what this is about, and send someone to do his work."

"Yes, sir. I'll see to it," Gideon replied.

As a couple of the cowboys rode away, Hardin swung down from his own mount. "I appreciate the help your men gave the timber camp a few days back."

Cutler's brow furrowed as he eyed the marshal. "Yeah, well, we're counting on those timber cutters ourselves—didn't want to see any of 'em killed. Vance had it coming when you locked him up for stealing from them. Zeke doesn't deserve this; he's ten times the man Vance ever was."

"Mr. Cutler, I promise you this: I'll make sure all the witnesses testify on Zeke's behalf," Hardin said. "I'm only following the law."

"We've gotten by with our own take on the law in the territory," Cutler admitted.

"That's why they sent me," Hardin replied. "The territorial governor, Charles Houten, wants lawbreakers held to account. Making sure criminals face justice will help push Montana toward statehood."

Cutler fell silent, his face impassive as he shook his head.

"Cattle thieves are plaguing Montana, Cutler—I've already collared one gang. You ought to be grateful Houten's bringing more law to the territory," Hardin pressed.

"I am, Marshal. It's just... I've seen the law go wrong too many times," Cutler explained, his voice laced with concern.

"That can happen, sure. But it's rare when there are solid witnesses."

"We'll see about that," Cutler said, his eyes flicking toward two riders approaching. "Zeke's coming now, Marshal."

Hardin swung into his saddle as the pair drew near. "Zeke, you're coming with me." He reined his horse alongside the young man's. "Hand over that gun, son."

Zeke unbuckled his holster and passed the six-shooter without a word, then turned to Cutler. "I'm sorry, Mr. Cutler. I know McCray would've killed me if I hadn't drawn my gun."

"Zeke, set that worry aside and tell the judge everything you told me," Cutler said firmly.

"Yes, sir."

"Where are you taking him, Marshal?" Cutler asked, his brow creased with concern.

"Miles City's got the nearest jail, and the judge lives just outside town," Hardin replied.

With that, Hardin wheeled his horse toward the main road, Zeke riding beside him as they left Cutler's ranch behind.

16

A light rain fell as Hardin and Zeke rode into Miles City. After dismounting, they tied their horses to the hitch rail and walked into the sheriff's office, where Shepard sat hunched over his desk, sifting through papers. He looked up as they came in.

"Who's this you've got with you?" Shepard asked, an eyebrow arched.

"This is Zeke Kane," Hardin replied. "He shot and killed a man at the saloon in Bitterroot Springs and needs to go before Judge Quinn."

Shepard nodded slowly. "In that case, I'll need you to fill out a form—give the judge the details for sentencing."

"I'm hoping the judge will hear the witnesses I've lined up," Hardin added. "They'll swear it was self-defense."

"If that's the truth of it, you ought to cut him loose, Marshal," Shepard replied, leaning back in his chair.

"The law says a judge has to hear the case first," Hardin said.

"Phooey on the law," Shepard shot back, his irritation plain. "I don't want to put an innocent man behind bars—it'll cost the town quite a lot."

"It has to be done. Plus, Zeke's got a horse and a rig that needs tending until he's out of jail," Hardin said.

"I can already tell, Marshal, you're gonna be a real pain in my backside," Shepard replied with a weary shake of his head.

Hardin handed over Zeke's gun. "Just lock him up, Sheriff."

Shepard drew in a deep breath, eyeing the young man with disdain. "Give me the rest of it, son—belt and all."

Zeke unbuckled his holster and passed it over. Shepard retrieved the key from the hook on the wall and led the way to the jail cells. "Take your pick—they're all empty," he said offhandedly.

Hardin glanced into the vacant row of cells, a spark of anger flaring up. "Where are the rustlers, Sheriff?" he demanded, his voice sharpening.

Shepard turned to face him, a flicker of unease settling on his features. "Uh, they escaped. I figured you knew about it."

"I haven't been anywhere near Miles City, so how would I? How in blazes did they pull that off?" Hardin pressed, his irritation sharpening.

"Well, a couple of women showed up with some food for them," Shepard said, easing the cell door shut behind Zeke. "One got too close to the bars, and a prisoner grabbed her. The other woman, scared for her friend, grabbed the keys off the peg and let 'em all loose."

"Of all the incompetence..." Hardin muttered, shaking his head. "How could you let this happen? You know better than to allow folks on the outside to feed prisoners—they don't understand the risks."

"I wasn't here," Shepard shot back defensively. "My deputy, Wade Norman, was minding the place. He's still learning the ropes."

"You need a replacement deputy. So, what are you doing to find the rustlers?" Hardin said with a sharp, demanding stare.

"I can't chase them outside the town's boundary. I'm not a marshal like you."

Hands on his hips, Hardin stood fuming. "Just hand over that paperwork and I'll fill it out, and see that it gets to the judge. This boy shouldn't be locked up, and he'd better be out soon."

Shepard fetched the form from a cabinet and slid it across the desk. "I'll run it over to Judge Quinn first thing, but my hands are tied till he rules on it."

"Tell him I'm sending those witnesses to Miles City straightaway." Hardin scrawled out the details on the form. "Well, I have a long ride ahead of me." He left the form lying on the desk.

Stepping quickly out of the sheriff's office, he swung into the saddle and guided Amos toward the general mercantile. A handful of ranch hands were out front, heaving sacks of feed into a wagon as he dismounted and secured the reins around the hitch rail.

One of the cowboys straightened up, then ambled over. "Howdy, Marshal. Name's Wylie Barton. You hear tell of any rustlers prowling these parts?"

"I have," Hardin said. "What do you know about them?"

"Two of my cowhands spotted five men rounding up our cattle yesterday. I gathered some boys and tracked 'em down. We exchanged gunfire and I'm pretty sure we winged one of 'em."

"I'll swing by the doc's and see if he's patched up any fresh gunshot wounds," Hardin replied.

"Marshal, we thought of that and checked with Dr. Burkes ourselves," Barton said. "Up till yesterday evening, he hadn't seen a soul with a bullet wound."

"I'll drop in on him again and check," Hardin replied. "If you need me, I'm riding back to Bitterroot Springs. Just wire me, and I'll come as quickly as I can."

"You bet. I laid it all out for Sheriff Shepard, but it didn't amount to spit."

"Bet he pulled out the jurisdiction excuse."

"You got it," Barton said as he climbed into the wagon. "I'll see you around, Marshal."

Hardin gave a nod and walked into the store.

"Mister, what can I do for you?" the balding storekeeper asked, wiping his hands on a stained white apron. Spotting the badge as Hardin turned, he quickly added, "I apologize, Marshal, didn't see the badge."

"No harm done. Name's Reuben Hardin."

"I'm pleased to meet you, Marshal. My name is Harold Wightman, and the missus—Rebecca's her name—is working in the back today. What can I do for you?"

"A couple of boxes of .45-75 cartridges and..."

"...the Centennial Model," Wightman cut in with a grin.

"That's right."

"I wasn't sure who snatched up that rifle, but now I know."

"Just the one you've stocked?" Hardin asked.

"Yes, sir. The company offered me a small discount to put it on the shelf. How do you like it so far?"

"I've only fired a box of bullets through it, but I think I'm going to enjoy it," Hardin replied.

Wightman set two boxes of cartridges on the counter. "What else do you need, Marshal?"

"Do you grind coffee beans?" Hardin asked.

"Yes, sir, grind it myself."

"Give me two pounds and a pound of sugar," Hardin said.

The older man weighed out the ground coffee and sugar, then placed them on the counter. "Here you are," he said. "That fella who just pulled out—Barton—he mentioned some cattle thieves hittin' his spread a few days back. Reckon they made off with a few head."

"I ran into him outside, and he filled me in," Hardin said.

"You got any notion who they might be, Marshal?"

"I've got a fair idea of a couple," Hardin replied, tiring of folks prying. "But that's not something I care to share just now, sir."

"Oh, I reckon you can't, at that," Wightman said.

Hardin paid for his supplies, stepped out into the crisp air, and mounted Amos, then headed to Dr. Burke's to inquire about men with bullet wounds. Satisfied with what he learned, he rode out of Miles City, realizing he wouldn't make Bitterroot Springs before nightfall unless he rode straight through.

Darkness crept in after hours on the trail, prompting him to make camp. Just as he stopped Amos to dismount, he spotted the dim silhouette of a covered wagon a ways ahead. Drawing nearer, he caught the faint sound of a child's voice.

"Hello, in the wagon! Everything all right?" Hardin called out, but only silence answered as he swung down from his horse. "I'm a U.S. Marshal. Anything I can do to help?"

A face peered from behind the wagon's canvas flap. "You really a marshal?" came a soft woman's voice.

"Yes, ma'am. You holding up alright?"

"I'm fine, but my husband has been shot."

Hardin approached the wagon and cautiously peered inside.

"Marshal, two men rode by and robbed us—they shot Henry," she explained, her voice trembling.

Hardin climbed up the back of the wagon to check the wound. "That's a bad one, ma'am. He needs a doctor to dig that bullet out."

The woman let out a soft whimper, dabbing at her tears with the hem of her dress. "He's gonna die, isn't he?"

"Not if we hurry and get him to a doctor," Hardin said. "What're your names?"

"My husband is Henry Baskin. I'm Hannah, and this is our son, Jeremiah," she replied, nodding toward the child huddled nearby.

"Hannah, I'll tie my horse to the back and drive your wagon. It's still about twenty miles to Bitterroot, and with dark coming on, we won't make good time—but we've got to get him to that doctor. Now, you will have to keep pressure on his wound to prevent more bleeding while we travel."

"Alright, Marshal. We're in your hands," Hannah said.

Hardin quickly secured Amos to the back of the wagon, climbed into the seat, and snapped the reins, setting the team in motion.

Mindful of the treacherous spots along the trail, Hardin maneuvered the wagon carefully.

As dawn drew near, he spotted a dim light through Dr. Hawkin's window as they approached. He reined the team to a halt near the porch and jumped down.

"Let me wake her," he said, walking toward the porch.

After several knocks on the door, he heard footsteps approaching.

"Who's there?" Dr. Hawkins called out.

"It's Marshal Hardin. I've got a man with a bullet wound."

The door swung open, and Dr. Hawkins stood there in her night robe. "Take him to the first room down the hallway. I'll be there in a minute."

Hardin retrieved Henry from the back of the wagon as Hannah pressed a cloth to the wound to stem the bleeding. Carrying the man through the front door, he laid him down on the operating table. He found a lantern and matches and lit it just as the doctor entered the room, dressed in a simple white gown.

Dr. Hawkins examined the bullet wound and turned to Hannah. "Are you the wife?" she asked.

"Yes."

"Hand your rag to Hardin. Go to the kitchen, find a large pot, and fill it with water. There's a water pump beside the cabinet. Bring it to a boil on the stove. You may need to stoke the fire, or it won't get hot enough."

Hannah stared at Victoria as she gazed at her husband, hesitating.

"If you want me to get that bullet out of him, you need to help," Victoria urged.

Hardin could see Hannah's reluctance to leave her husband. "I'll take care of it, Doctor. She should stay with her husband."

As Hardin headed to the kitchen, Dr. Hawkins gathered her surgical tools and arranged them on a tray beside the operating table. She then turned to a cabinet and retrieved a couple of bottles of chloroform and alcohol.

"What's that for?" Hannah asked.

"The chloroform will keep him asleep," Dr. Hawkins explained. "When I start extracting that bullet, he's likely to wake up. It's better to keep him unconscious during the surgery."

"What about the other bottle?"

"It's for cleaning the wound to prevent infection."

Dr. Hawkins turned as Hardin entered the room carrying a large pan of hot water, which he carefully set down on the floor. "Marshal, please find another pan and pour about half of the hot water into it," she instructed.

Once Hardin divided the water, Dr. Hawkins washed her hands in one of the pans and began to dig for the bullet. "Hannah, you should wait in the other room while I finish him."

"But I want to stay," Hannah protested.

Dr. Hawkins considered her request. "Alright, you can stand to the side, but I don't want any distractions."

Within a few minutes, Dr. Hawkins successfully extracted the bullet and dropped it into a glass jar. Then she cleaned the wound and applied alcohol before stitching it closed.

"Hannah, you can pull up a chair and sit with your husband. I'll check on him shortly," Dr. Hawkins said before turning to leave the room.

Hardin pursued her into the kitchen. "You did great work for that man," he commented as she washed her hands. "He may still live."

"Did you shoot him, Marshal?" Victoria asked, raising an eyebrow.

"No, it wasn't me," Hardin replied. "Hanna said they ran into a couple of men who robbed them. Her husband grabbed his shotgun to intervene when they shot him."

After drying her hands on a towel, Victoria took a seat at the table.

"You look tired," Hardin said.

"I suppose I am. It was a long day before this—they called me to help with a childbirth," she explained, and smiled. "But it's not your fault that I chose to become a doctor."

"Maybe not," Hardin replied. "I still can't understand why you'd choose to practice medicine in this rugged wilderness when you could have been a doctor in an eastern city where there is better law enforcement."

"I suppose you wouldn't. Marshal, how about coming over for dinner one evening?" Victoria suggested.

"When?" Hardin inquired.

She gazed at him, lost in thought, her eyes fixed on his face. "Well, tomorrow I have a surgery scheduled, but the day after should work."

Hardin raised an eyebrow with a slight grin. "I'll do my best. Like you, I often find myself with last-minute commitments."

"Try to come, please. We'll swap stories."

He smiled as he stood up. "I'd like that. But for the moment, I've got other matters to attend to."

She tilted her head and remarked, "Yes, I know, the busy life of a marshal." As he made his way to the door, she kept her gaze on him. *He's quite the man.*

17

The sun glared through the window of the up-stairs hotel room where Hardin lay in bed, yearning for more sleep. When it didn't come, he swung his legs over the side and sat up, gazing out the window at the bustling main street of Bitterroot Springs. The scene below was lively with horse-drawn wagons, cow-boys, and locals browsing the few shops for various items. Men came and went from the barbershop, while women found their way to the local dress shop. Others gathered at the Lonesome Pine Cafe and the general store.

"Looks like it's shaping up to be a busy day in 'Bitter Land'. I suppose I should do my part," Hardin murmured to himself.

He slipped into his britches, buttoned his shirt, and tucked it in neatly. After putting on his hat and strapping on his revolver, he stepped from his room and hurried down the stairs. Giving a quick wave to the clerk at the counter, he headed outside, ready to face the day's activities.

As Hardin pushed open the café door, he could see it was lunchtime in the small town as every table looked occupied. Then he saw Mayor Barlow seated alone on the other side of the room.

Barlow looked up as Hardin approached. "Hello, Marshal. It seems there's not much room today. Would you care to join me?" he offered.

"I was hoping you'd say that," Hardin replied, appreciating the invitation.

"Of course. I always welcome a visit from our marshal," Barlow remarked with a smile.

As Hardin settled at the table, Darcy West spotted him and made her way over. "Hey, Marshal. Would you like today's special? We have pork chops, brown beans, and potato soup."

"That sounds good to me, along with a glass of tea," Hardin answered.

Darcy stepped away from the table, and Barlow paused to sip his tea. Setting the glass down, he remarked, "Marshal, I heard you caught some rustlers red-handed."

"That's right," Hardin responded. "Unfortunately, the sheriff over at Miles City let them escape."

"How does something like that happen?" Barlow asked, raising an eyebrow.

"Does it really matter how? They're gone and could start stealing cattle again. We were fortunate the first time that a cowhand spotted them," Hardin replied.

"Maybe another will, too, but what will you do until then, Marshal?"

"I'll listen for another lead and then go after them, which reminds me of a matter I need to discuss with you."

"And what might that be?" Barlow inquired.

"About getting a sheriff for Bitterroot Springs. This town is in as much need of a lawman as Miles City is," Hardin declared, "with the fort nearby, plus all the ranch hands. You have both cowboys and soldiers stirring trouble, and I'm called on to deal with them.

If you had a sheriff for the town business, I could focus on tracking down cattle rustlers and settling disputes between timber cutters and ranch owners. As it stands, I'm spending more time in the saddle than I am solving crimes."

Barlow set down his fork and wiped his mouth with a towel as the waitress set Hardin's lunch on the table.

"Is there anything else, Marshal?" Darcy asked.

"This is fine, Darcy," Hardin replied.

As Darcy walked away to assist another table, Barlow turned to Hardin. "I've been working on getting a sheriff, Marshal. I thought I made that quite clear."

"Yeah, you mentioned it, Mayor, but the fact remains you still don't have one—or a jail. I had to take a prisoner to Miles City yesterday. If we had a sheriff and a jail, the judge would be required to come to Bitterroot."

Barlow offered an agreeing nod. "It's not that I don't see your point, but I have concerns about the candidates who have shown interest in the job."

Hardin paused to chew his food before continuing. "You're right to be cautious about who you hire, but you've got to put in more effort. Expand your search, offer competitive pay, and give your sheriff the authority to operate outside of town when necessary. Building a jailhouse will go a long way toward attracting. No lawman will want to come to Bitterroot Springs if there's no place to detain prisoners."

"Alright, I'll talk it over with the city council," Barlow replied. "They also want a sheriff of top quality. However, the council might hesitate about that jailhouse."

"Well, remind them that there's a sawmill here that can provide the lumber," Hardin added.

"Right, I will do that."

Hardin paused, taking a bite, and met Barlow's gaze once again. "I trust you haven't forgotten that you promised to be a witness in the Zeke Kane case."

"Oh, of course not. Let me think..." Barlow rubbed his chin, pondering.

"Barlow, you have to testify, or Judge Quinn could hang an innocent man," Hardin urged.

"I will go, but I just need to determine when."

"If you don't in the next two days, it could be too late for Zeke Kane. The young man acted in self-defense when he shot the McCray boy and deserves to be exonerated," Hardin said, his frustration mounting.

"There were others from the saloon who witnessed the shooting, Marshal. You should have one of them testify," Barlow suggested.

"If you back out of this and an innocent man is hanged, don't ever expect me to do you a favor again," Hardin retorted sharply.

Barlow's eyes widened as he realized the depth of Hardin's displeasure. "Alright, I'll go tomorrow. I'm not looking forward to that long buggy ride, but I'll do it."

Hardin took a sip of tea and held his glass out in front of him. "I'll send a telegram to the sheriff at Miles City to verify your statement."

Barlow swallowed. "You... you don't have to concern yourself, Marshal. I'll get it done." He turned and walked away from Hardin's table, exiting the café.

As Hardin watched Barlow leave, he wondered how someone could let an innocent man suffer for defending himself. Zeke Kane deserved his freedom from jail, and he vowed to make it happen. Tom Carson had also agreed to testify, but Hardin was unsure where to find him. He hoped Charles Stewart at the general store might have some leads, or perhaps one of the bank tellers could help. It was crucial to locate Carson before Zeke Kane faced the noose. He couldn't trust Barlow to follow through with what he'd said.

18

Barlow convinced the city council to build a jailhouse and later summoned Hardin to share his insights on the project. They agreed on a two-room log-style structure, with one room designated as the office and the other for the jail cells.

"Well, gentlemen, if we're finished here," Hardin said, "I have other matters to attend to."

"Of course," Barlow replied. "But would you mind stopping by occasionally to check their progress? Your oversight will help ensure that everything is proceeding as it should."

"Sure, I can do that."

A cowboy suddenly walked into Barlow's office. "I hate to interrupt, but I need to speak with the marshal."

"What's happened?" Hardin asked.

"A couple of cowboys from Amos Cutler's ranch got into it, and one of them was shot. We're heading to the doctor to get him patched up, and thought you ought to know."

"What's your name?" Hardin asked as he stepped outside.

"Caleb Holt," he said, gesturing to the injured man lying in the back of the buckboard. "My buddy there, Obie Judd, is the one who got shot."

"Take the road toward Miles City. Her place is on the left. I'll ride along with you," Hardin said and then mounted his horse.

They reached Dr. Hawkins' residence, and the two men carried the injured cowboy to the door. Hardin knocked, and when there was no answer, he reached for the doorknob and found it unlocked.

As they stepped inside, the marshal called out, "Dr. Hawkins, are you here?"

No one responded, so Hardin and Caleb carried Obie to the surgery table. As they carefully laid him down, Dr. Hawkins stepped out from around the corner.

"I'm sorry for the holdup," she said. "I was outside working on the house. What's happened to him?"

"He's got a bullet in him, ma'am," Caleb explained. "It's in the side of his guts."

"Keep pressure on the wound with this," the doctor instructed, handing him a towel. "We have to make sure he doesn't bleed anymore. I'll return shortly after I clean up."

Dr. Hawkins brushed against Hardin as she passed by. "Didn't expect to see you so soon."

He grinned, his eyes following her as she left the room.

Caleb glanced at his friend, lying unconscious on the table. "I hope she can remove that slug, Marshal."

"I believe she can," Hardin assured. "I've seen her work firsthand. I need you to tell me what happened."

"It was Tim Forde who shot him. Do you think Forde will have to go to jail?"

"If Obie dies, he very well might," Hardin replied. "I'll need all the facts before I can say for certain."

"Okay, sure."

Dr. Hawkins stepped into the room wearing a white coat.

"You look important, ma'am," Caleb remarked.

"Just doing what I can to keep the wound clean," Dr. Hawkins responded. "And please, call me Doctor, not ma'am."

"Yes, ma'am—I mean, Doctor," Caleb corrected himself.

Dr. Hawkins then directed Caleb to the waiting area while Hardin assisted her. In just a few moments, she had removed the bullet, cleaned the wound, and sutured it. "You can tell that cowboy he can come in now," she said.

Caleb walked into the room and gazed nervously at his friend lying unconscious on the table. "Is he going to make it, Doctor?"

"I believe he will," Dr. Hawkins replied. "You did well by stopping the bleeding. If you'd like to stay with him, that would be perfectly fine."

Caleb shook his head. "My boss might not be too happy about that. I'd better head back to the ranch."

"Caleb, Obie will be fine here until he's back on his feet."

"Thanks," Caleb said and headed toward the door.

"Caleb, do you know a cowboy named Tom Carson?" Hardin inquired.

"Oh, sure. Tom's my foreman," Caleb answered.

"I'll ride along with you to the ranch," Hardin said as they walked toward the horses. "I need a word with him."

"Marshal," Dr. Hawkins called out. "Can I still expect you tonight?"

He nodded. "I'll be here, unless a range war breaks out." He turned Amos and rode away with Caleb in the buckboard.

Hiram Steele clung to the saddle horn of the gray mare as he attempted to green break her. Determined not to fall after hitting the ground five times already, he dug into her sides with his boot heels. The mare made another turn in the round pen, bucking and snorting, until she once again unseated the cowboy.

Hiram pulled off his hat and slammed it into the dirt. "That's one tough gray nag."

Rufus Clay ran after the mare, grabbed the loose reins, and tried to calm her down. "You'll get her, Hiram. Just give her one more round."

"I won't be able to walk after one more round," Hiram replied, frustration in his voice.

Rufus glanced toward the ranch house as two riders approached. "Caleb's back."

Rising to his feet, Hiram faced the ranch house. "I don't see Obie with them."

"You reckon he didn't make it?" Obie asked.

"It looks like that marshal from town came too," Hiram said. "I wonder what's up?"

Hardin and Caleb dismounted, then Caleb headed inside the ranch house. A few moments later, an older man wearing suspenders, blue britches, and a button-down shirt followed Caleb out to the porch.

Hardin removed his hat and extended his hand to the man. "Are you Amos Cutler?" he asked.

"I am," the man replied. "I'm usually at the bank, but since my men have some cattle to move, I figured I should stay close."

"Can you tell me what you know about the gunfight?" Hardin inquired.

"Well, those two men had been at each other for days," Cutler explained. "My foreman, Tom Carson, told me it started in the saloon over a woman. On the day of the gunfight, Obie was prodding Tim, and I reckon Tim finally had enough. He called Obie out, and they headed to the corral." Cutler gestured toward the round pen where they broke horses. "They stood there for a while before one of them drew his pistol. Tim was faster and shot Obie in the side."

"Did you notice who drew first?" Hardin asked.

"Most of the men thought it was Tim," Cutler responded. "I let him go after they put Obie in the wagon. We can't have gunplay around here—neither at the ranch nor among those who work for us."

"I wish you'd let me take him in," Hardin said. "If Obie dies, I'll need to track Tim down for murder."

"I understand, Marshal," Cutler replied. "But Obie looked like he might pull through, so I decided to let Tim go. I'm sorry if that was a mistake."

"I'll deal with him," Hardin said, "but I also came to find Tom Carson."

"Carson?" Cutler asked, his brow furrowing. "I know Tom isn't perfect, and maybe drinks a little too much, but surely he hasn't done anything to warrant being taken in."

"No, I need him to testify about another shooting," Hardin replied.

"You're referring to the incident from the saloon."

"That's right, Mr. Cutler. I'm trying to prevent a man from being hanged for defending himself."

"If you need Tom, you can have him," Cutler offered.

"Would you mind asking him to come to town in the morning to see me?" Hardin requested. "I need him to ride to Miles City."

"That will take 2–3 days. What am I supposed to do?" Cutler complained.

"I know it will, but it's necessary to save a man's life."

"Would a judge accept his testimony on paper?" Cutler asked.

"I believe so—he accepted mine. Have Tom ride to Bitterroot Springs in the morning with it written out. He can find me at the hotel or the café."

"Alright, Marshal, I'll send him out. By the way, how is Obie doing?"

"Dr. Hawkins removed the bullet and patched him up. She said he just needs plenty of rest to heal and regain his strength."

Cutler nodded. "I haven't had the chance to meet her."

Hardin mounted his horse and looked down at the rancher. "But don't meet her on the operating table when you do."

With a grin, Cutler replied, "I certainly won't try that, Marshal."

19

After the ride from Amos Cutler's ranch and all the challenges Hardin had faced during the week, he managed to sleep for a few hours, hoping he'd feel up to going to Dr. Hawkins' place for supper.

He asked the hotel staff to prepare a warm bath before he shaved. As he slipped on his clean britches, his thoughts wandered to the new doctor. There was an air of mystery about her arrival in this small town. Perhaps something had gone awry with a patient, or maybe she had found it difficult to collaborate with male doctors—he had heard tales of doctors' outright disdain for working alongside a woman. Whatever the cause, Victoria seemed reluctant to share her story.

Hardin combed his hair and applied a hint of cologne he had purchased from the barber, though he couldn't shake the idea that it might cause him to smell flowery.

After leaving the hotel and getting his horse from the livery, he made his way out of town.

Victoria spotted Hardin as he rode up and directed him to a corral she had paid a man to build. He unsaddled Amos, released him into the enclosure, and then headed toward the house.

Hardin approached the back of the residence and met Victoria at the back steps. "I didn't know you had a corral," he said.

"A man from town built it for me," Victoria replied. "He and another man are also fencing off a few acres so I can have a horse."

"You ride?" Hardin asked.

"I do," Victoria responded. "But I'll mostly use mine for pulling a buggy. Come in."

They went inside, and she led Hardin to the kitchen.

Victoria turned to tend to the cooking. "You can stay in here if you'd like while I finish up with the food. The stove got hotter than I expected and slowed me down."

"I'm easy to please, so don't worry about me," Hardin replied. "By the way, how is the young cowboy with the bullet wound doing?"

"Obie? He's back at the ranch where he works," Victoria answered, turning back to the stove. "I had hoped he'd stay here a few more days to let that wound heal properly, but cowboys are a stubborn lot."

"He'll come back if he has any problems."

"Yeah, let's hope he does. Well, I think the food is finally ready," Victoria said. "Could you carry a couple of things to the dining table?"

Hardin stood from his chair, picked up a platter and a bowl, and made his way to the dining room. He set the food down and looked around the room. "Doctor, this is one of the finest dining rooms I've ever seen."

"That's very kind of you to say," Victoria replied.

She directed Hardin to an end seat at the table and chose one nearest to him. "If it's alright with you, I'd like to bless the food."

"Be my guest," he said.

After she prayed, they enjoyed their supper, engaging in light conversation about the local news in Bitterroot.

Once finished with his meal, Hardin pushed back his chair. "That was excellent. You're truly a woman of many talents."

"Thank you. My mother never expected me to become a doctor, so she taught me to cook," Victoria replied, standing to gather their plates. "I'll just take these to the kitchen."

She returned with a box of cigars and offered him one.

"I've never taken up tobacco," Hardin said.

"What about a quirly?" Victoria asked.

"A quirly? That's hand-rolled Bull Durham tobacco, right? No, I haven't since the Civil War," Hardin replied. "I always worried that buying it might make folks think I supported slavery. What about you, Doctor? There has to be more to your move to this rugged, wild Montana than just a chance to work in a small town."

"Victoria—call me Victoria. We know each other well enough to use first names, don't you think?" she said.

"Sure. I don't mind."

"To answer your question, Reuben, after receiving my medical degree, I found no opportunities in New York. People there aren't quite ready for a female doctor. While a few manage, they often struggle to attract enough patients."

"You might face the same here in Bitterroot Springs," Hardin replied.

"I'm sure that's true, but I'm currently the only qualified doctor available. People will have to travel all the way to Miles City or come to see me," she said, looking into his eyes. "What about you? Surely, you could find a marshal or sheriff's position in Missouri, Kansas, or even Texas. What's your real reason for coming to Bitterroot Springs?"

There it was, Hardin thought—the question he preferred to avoid. If only the past could stay buried? "Um, I was a sheriff in Hays City, Kansas. I managed to clean up the town and drive out the criminals." He paused, searching for the right words. "I've taken men's lives—some while serving in Hays City, others during the war—but none haunt me like the night I killed a fourteen-year-old in a dark alley. That night, we heard someone firing shots in the street. My deputy and I walked down the alley, calling for him to stop and come out. He jumped up from behind a barrel and fired at me. I reacted like any lawman would and returned fire. All we could see were the flashes from his gun and his silhouette; he looked so much older than his years before he fell to the ground."

"I'm sorry," Victoria said gently. "That's such a heartbreaking story."

"Well, anyway, the city council let me go as their sheriff. I looked for other jobs as a sheriff because that's all I ever wanted to be. A friend of mine, who is the director of the U.S. Marshals Service, encouraged me to come here. He pulled some strings to help me secure the position because of the incident in Hays City. I'll have to stay until he decides I've been here long enough, but I hope that my work here will serve as a solid résumé for a job elsewhere."

Victoria looked at him with curiosity. "Is there a woman in your life, Reuben?" she asked.

"There have been a few over the years," Hardin replied. "I once thought I would marry a woman while I was in Hays City, but my constant confrontations with criminals and gunfighters gave her pause."

Victoria nodded as she rose from her chair. "That's the challenge with jobs that serve people—you often have no time for a relationship." She took a few steps toward Hardin and settled down in his lap. Wrapping her arms around him, she said, "You and I are on equal footing. Perhaps there's a chance for us to find something good in this." She leaned in and kissed him softly for a moment before pulling back with a smile.

"Perhaps we can," Hardin replied.

"If you'd like to sleep in the extra bedroom..." she said. "I have plenty of room here."

Hardin gazed into her deep brown eyes, reflecting on his Christian upbringing. He had always been cautious in relationships, determined not to tarnish his reputation. He also had to consider Victoria's status as a doctor. "I appreciate the gesture, but I'd better not. You have an image to uphold, just as I do."

She kissed him again. "Then you'll have to make an effort to visit me often, and I don't mean only when you bring in a gunshot victim."

"I'll do my best," he said. "But I need to get up early in the morning. I would like to follow up with a couple of witnesses who have promised to testify on behalf of a man currently in the Miles City jail. So, I should be on my way."

Victoria embraced him tightly, kissing his neck several times before moving to his lips and sharing a long, lingering kiss. Finally, she pulled away, taking a deep breath. "Maybe those will hold me for a while." With that, she rose from his lap.

Hardin stood and placed his hat on his head, surprised that such a stunning woman would be interested in him. In his mind, he wasn't overly attractive and even bore a small scar across one side of his face. Yet, he understood that women often find qualities in men that they themselves frequently overlooked.

He wrapped his arms around her and said, "I'm guessing you want a horse and buggy for more than just trips into town."

"That's right," Victoria replied. "I've had patients who can hardly make it here when I need to see them. I want to make rounds to their homes and make sure they are following the medications and treatments I prescribed."

"I hope you realize how unsafe it is for anyone to travel the trails out of Bitterroot Springs," he said. "I came across some Indians a while back, and I'm sure you remember the people from the wagon some wicked men attacked."

"I understand the risks, but my patients need me," Victoria replied. "I can shoot a gun—I actually have two: a shotgun and a revolver."

Victoria was a woman who forged her own path, and he knew nothing he said would change her mind. Still, this knowledge added another layer of worry for him. "Alright then. I'd better get Amos saddled and head back so I can rest."

"You'll need a lamp since it's dark. I'll carry it," Victoria said.

"I appreciate that," Hardin replied as he began to walk toward the door.

Once he had saddled his horse, he led it through the gate and turned to Victoria. "Do you ever get to town to eat?"

"I haven't yet," she answered. "But once my buggy arrives, I will." She leaned in and kissed him once more before he mounted up.

"I'll see you soon," Hardin said.

"Goodbye, Reuben," she replied, watching him ride away.

20

Abe Tucker, the telegraph operator, shuffled through a stack of papers as Hardin waited beside him. He took a paper from the pile and turned to the marshal. "I believe this is what you're after. It's from Sheriff Bud Shepard at Miles City," he said.

Hardin read the return message, which confirmed that Tom Carson and Glenn Barlow had testified on behalf of Zeke Kane, and Shepard released the young cowboy. "Thank you," Hardin said, stepping out onto the porch.

He glanced across the street, where construction of the new jail had begun. Three men laid out strings and stakes for the foundation, as they measured the distance to each corner. As Hardin watched them working, Abe Tucker stepped out the door behind him.

"Marshal, you'd better come back in. I've got another message coming in for you," Abe said.

Once Abe finished writing the message, he tore off the sheet and handed it to Hardin. "This one is from the mayor of Miles City."

The telegram read: *Please inform the new marshal that the stage leaving Miles City toward Bitterroot Springs was attacked by Indians. A cowboy witnessed the incident from a distance but said it was too late to help. It's important you know the Indians killed everyone on board, burned the stage, and are headed toward Bitterroot Springs. Marshal, I also sent a telegram to the army at Fort Miles requesting their help, because some of the passengers were citizens of Miles City.*

"I've got to go," Hardin said, still pondering the message. He exited the telegraph office and made his way to the livery. After saddling Amos, he rode quickly out of town.

Several miles out of town, gunfire caught Hardin's attention, and he slowed his pace. As he drew closer, he noticed army troopers engaged in a gun battle with Indians. He secured Amos to a tree, safe from the conflict, and worked his way through the woods until he spotted a man in a blue uniform.

"How many are there, corporal?" Hardin asked.

"We believe there are seven," the corporal replied. "A group of Blackfeet who have left the reservation. We may have already killed three of them."

Hardin drew his gun and positioned himself alongside the corporal.

"You're that new marshal I've heard about," the corporal said.

"Reuben Hardin. It's a pleasure to meet you," Hardin replied.

He nodded. "Silas McCready. Likewise."

As Hardin spotted an Indian attempting to break away from the others to his right, he called out, "I'm going after the one over here, so don't shoot me."

"I won't," Corporal McCready assured.

The Indian had taken to the ground to crawl, inching his way toward a trooper who was oblivious to his presence. Hardin advanced cautiously, using the trees for cover. He was about twenty feet away when the Indian suddenly turned and saw him. As the Indian rolled onto his back and aimed his rifle, Hardin shot, hitting him twice.

The gunfire continued for several minutes as the soldiers kept shooting at the remaining three Indians. Finally, with their backs against a straight up hill and the army surrounding them, one of the Indians raised his rifle and hands into the air, signaling his surrender.

"Hold your fire, men," Corporal McCready commanded.

Eleven Army troopers quickly surrounded the Indians, disarming them. The sergeant then ordered his men to secure their hands and put them on their horses.

"Corporal, I noticed that you got here pretty fast," Hardin remarked, watching the scene.

"Someone sent word about an hour ago that the stage had been attacked," Corporal Cready replied. "All the passengers were dead, the stage burned, and we found the Indians camped next to the river, checking out the things they had stolen."

While they were engaged in conversation, an Indian wearing an army uniform walked up beside them. "Marshal, this man is our tracker, Takoda Redleaf," Corporal Cready said. "He rode ahead of us and found them so that we could sneak up on them."

Hardin turned to the Indian and said, "Thanks for your help."

"They too easy. I heard them before I see them," Takoda replied.

Hardin gave them a nod. "Well, Corporal, they can't hurt anyone else. What happens to them now that you've captured them?"

"We'll take them to the reservation, and they'd better stay put this time," Corporal Cready responded.

"Give them food and blankets, they will stay," Takoda suggested.

"Takoda's right, Marshal," the corporal said. "The government doesn't always keep its promises to the Indians. They wouldn't jump the reservation if they gave them what they needed."

"Does the government realize this?" Hardin inquired.

"Oh, they're aware. Colonel Miles has sent several telegrams and letters to Washington. They make many promises, but nothing changes," Corporal Cready responded. "They really need to come here and see this for themselves."

"Perhaps someday things will change," Hardin said.

"Don't count on it," the corporal replied. "The Sioux, Arapaho, and some other tribes are gathering for a powwow. We believe they're planning more raids on farms and wagons. With so many tribes in one place, could be they are preparing for something huge. Colonel Miles told me that Colonel George Custer is organizing a large campaign with over 600 soldiers. Maybe that will resolve our problem once and for all."

Hardin remembered his trip to Montana and how the Indians attacked him. They were tough fighters, as skilled in their tactics, and more resilient than the army. "I hope you're right. Well, I should head back to Bitterroot Springs. Got some rustlers I need to track down."

"Marshal, I don't envy your task. Farewell, and thank you for your help."

"Of course, Corporal. I'll see you around."

He mounted Amos and set off toward Bitterroot Springs.

21

Hardin rode into Bitterroot Springs and dismounted at the livery, where Ezra Tate met him to take his horse.

"Marshal, a man's been asking around for you," Ezra said as he turned the horse toward the stable door. "He's been combing the town, trying to track you down."

"What does he want?" Hardin asked curiously as he followed along.

Ezra paused and met Hardin's gaze. "From the look of him and that gun he wears, I'd say he's out to kill somebody."

"Hmm, I wonder what this is all about?" Hardin mused.

"I don't know. Maybe you arrested one of his kin," Ezra suggested.

"I suppose I'd better find out. I'll see you later, Ezra."

Hardin figured that if the man were a gun-fighter, he'd most likely be at the saloon, but he decided to check a few spots along the way just to be thorough.

He walked to the café first, peering through the window to see an elderly couple quietly enjoying their coffee. Finding no one suspicious, he moved on to the general store, where the patrons browsing didn't match the description he'd heard, so he continued his search. The next two places were unlikely spots for a man of that sort, being people's homes. Finally, he arrived at the newspaper office and glanced through the window, spotting Sarah Harlan feeding paper into the printing press, but there was no sign of the gunfighter.

Then a voice rang out from across the street: "Marshal Hardin, I've been waiting for you!"

Hardin spun around to face the source, spotting a man dressed in a black hat, dark vest, and britches under a frock coat. The tell-tale bulge at his waist, hidden beneath the right side of his coat, left no doubt that this was the man who'd been asking after him.

Hardin stepped down from the board-walk and approached cautiously. "What's your name?" he asked.

"Jasper Kincaid," he replied, his voice gritty and determined, "and I'm here for you, Marshal,"

"What's this about?" Hardin pressed, a mix of curiosity and caution in his tone. "I don't know you."

"That don't matter much, does it?" Kincaid retorted, a slight smirk playing at the corners of his mouth.

Hardin scanned the street warily, noting a small crowd gathering at the cross street and another waiting near the bank, among them Sheriff Shepard, his deputy, and Mayor Barlow. "So, someone's paying for a gunman to do their dirty work?" Hardin remarked.

"That's right," Kincaid replied, a smirk playing on his lips as he eyed his opponent. "Though I'm not sure taking you out will do much for my reputation—you're not exactly known for your skill with a gun. Except maybe around these parts; I've done some checking.

I'll take money from anyone to go up against a man like you."

"Are you gonna tell me who it is?" Hardin probed.

Kincaid smiled wider, his tone dripping with intimidation. "Who's paying for it don't matter none. The only thing that does is you dying, Marshal."

"Aren't you forgetting something?" Hardin countered, his tone steady.

Kincaid's brows furrowed in confusion, his eyes narrowing as he shifted his weight. "What do you mean, Marshal?" he asked, a hint of defensiveness in his voice.

"You haven't seen me draw, so you don't really know how fast I am," Hardin replied calmly. "You're basing a gunfight on someone else's word, which means you're stepping into this street basically blindfolded. I thought gun-hands made it a point to observe their opponent before facing them."

"Yeah, I've done that with most of those I killed, but it's not necessary every time," Kincaid shot back, stepping further into the middle of the street as his bravado increased, a smirk tugging at his lips. "You see, I ain't met a lawman yet that I couldn't take."

"What if I decided not to draw on you?" Hardin asked.

Kincaid's eyes blazed with defiance, his stance wide as he positioned himself thirty to forty feet away from Hardin. "You'll draw, or you'll die!" he retorted. "But before that happens, I'll take out several townsfolk just to prove to you I mean what I say."

"Come on now, there's no reason for innocent people to get hurt," Hardin replied. "I'm the one you really want."

Kincaid chuckled, his yellowed teeth gleaming in the harsh sunlight as he pulled back his frock coat with a theatrical flourish, holding it aside to expose his holstered gun. "I thought you'd see it my way. Killing you will make me a lot of money."

As the gunfighter stared him down with unyielding intensity, Hardin slowly unlatched the thong from his Colt .45, positioning his hand over the weapon without once breaking eye contact. "You don't have to do this, Kincaid."

A grin twisted across Kincaid's face, his eyes glinting with determination. "Oh, but I do, Marshal. I've already received half the payment. I just need to finish the job and collect the rest."

Hardin stood steady and unflinching. "The problem is, you still think you'll get out of this alive."

"I intend to. So you'd better get ready!" Kincaid replied, his expression darkening with a surge of anger as he squared his shoulders.

Realizing that further conversation was pointless, Hardin fell silent, his gaze locked on the gunman's eyes.

Kincaid let an amused chuckle escape his lips—a familiar tactic to unsettle his opponents before a draw—but he struggled to gauge Hardin, whose expression remained as unmovable as stone.

Minutes ticked by as they locked eyes in a tense standoff, the street hanging heavy with anticipation. Finally, Kincaid decided he had waited long enough. His hand darted for his Smith & Wesson Model 3 Schofield, but Hardin was a split second faster, drawing his

Colt with precision and firing a single shot that struck Kincaid squarely in the chest.

Hardin kept his gun trained on the gunman as he crumpled to the ground, his eyes glazing over with a distant, unfocused stare. Kincaid's hat slipped down, partially obscuring his face, until Hardin kicked it aside with a boot.

"I'm sorry, Kincaid. I never wanted this," Hardin said quietly, unsure if the words reached the fading man.

With a final, rattling gasp, the gunfighter's chest heaved before falling silent, his lifeless body sprawled in the dirt—a stark reminder of the Gittens boy who had died by Hardin's hand, a weight he would always bear. This time, however, the confrontation had been driven by a genuine cause, one that justified the cost.

As Mayor Barlow and several townsfolk gathered around the fallen figure, Hardin scanned the crowd, his gaze sharpening when he spotted Victoria among them.

"Marshal, this is a terrible ordeal that happened here today," Barlow said with concern as he surveyed the crowd.

Hardin shot him a firm look. "I didn't start this, Mayor, and I tried my best to get out of it."

Barlow's brow furrowed skeptically. "I'm not convinced you tried hard enough."

Hardin's jaw tightened as the murmurs from the gathering crowd grew louder, fueling his frustration. "I'll say this once more so you folks will understand. This man was going to hurt some of you if I hadn't fought him—he came ready to die or be killed."

"He's right, people," Eli Whitaker, the undertaker, interjected. "I was standing right across from them the whole time—I heard every word. The marshal did everything he could to get that man to back down, but he wouldn't listen."

"Mayor, that's exactly what I witnessed," Dr. Hawkins added, her eyes locking steadily on the marshal with a nod of affirmation.

Hardin turned his gaze to Victoria and Eli. "Will you both fill out an affidavit for the judge?"

They nodded in agreement, and Hardin gestured for them to follow him toward the hotel.

As they walked down the street, Victoria glanced at Hardin, "I'm truly sorry this happened. It must be one of the hardest parts of your job."

Hardin let out a quiet sigh, managing a faint smile. "And there are other things I prefer to avoid." He shifted the conversation, his tone growing more serious. "So, you both heard what Kincaid said about being paid, right?"

"Heard it clear as day," Eli replied, shaking his head in disbelief. "It's hard to believe that someone paid to have you killed, Marshal. I could see Cornelius Vance behind it, but he's locked up in jail."

"Perhaps Vance has friends or family willing to settle scores on his behalf," Victoria suggested.

"Anything is possible," Hardin replied, clearly weighing their words.

Once they had completed the affidavit, Hardin bid the undertaker farewell and escorted Victoria to the café. They ordered coffee and settled at a quiet table by the window.

Barely a moment after they sat down, the café door burst open, and a lanky cowboy named Gordon Slade rushed in. "Marshal, sorry to interrupt, but there's a brawl breaking out in the saloon, and the bartender's asking for your help."

Hardin let out a weary sigh, setting his coffee cup down. "A lawman can't even enjoy his brew in peace." He turned to Victoria with a regretful nod. "I apologize, and I wish I could stay longer."

"Maybe next time, Reuben," Victoria replied.

"Yeah, maybe next time." Hardin put on his hat and headed for the door.

22

Hardin rolled over in bed, tugging the blanket over his head to block out the morning light. Ezra Tate was busy putting new shoes on Amos that morning, and Hardin hoped to steal a few more moments of sleep. Yet, after what seemed like only an hour of rest, he reluctantly swung his legs over the side of the bed.

Glancing at himself in the mirror, he ran his fingers through his hair, grimacing at the reflection. "Looks terrible. Better keep the hat on," he muttered to himself.

After washing his face, hands, and arms, he dried them with the hotel towel. Slowly, he slipped his britches on, then stepped to the window, peering outside to take in the morning scene. As he gazed out at the bustling street below, he recalled the previous night and its unusual peace—no fights erupting in the saloon or cattle rustling, and even the ranch-ers were uncharacteristically quiet. Thankful-ly, the night had passed without the interrup-tion of his recurring nightmare, confirming they were his obstacle to a good night's rest.

Out the window, his eyes caught the café door swinging open, and Lydia stepped outside with an elderly woman. She helped her into a buggy while her husband made his way to the other side. Hardin couldn't help but admire Lydia's gentle heart.

Their presence at the café reminded him that his stomach was calling for food. After slipping on his shirt and securing his gun, he grabbed his hat and headed out the door.

He arrived to find a couple sitting at a table and another man dining alone, quietly enjoy-ing breakfast. His extra moment of sleep had allowed most of the other patrons to finish their meals and move on.

Taking a seat, he noticed Darcy West ap-proaching with a welcoming smile. "Darling, what will it be?" she asked.

"Ham and eggs, biscuits and coffee," Hardin replied.

"Sure, I'll place your order and bring you some coffee."

"Thanks, Darcy."

Lydia emerged from the kitchen with a plate for the man seated alone, carefully setting it down on his table. After satisfying the patron, she turned and made her way toward Hardin.

Despite Lydia's alluring appearance, her true nature remained a mystery. He recalled that her early years were filled with hardship, making it difficult for her to move forward without a significant other to lend a hand. But her determination in the face of adversity was part of what drew him to her.

She took a seat across from the marshal. "Hardin, we really got off on the wrong foot, but can we start again?" she asked, her voice wavering.

"I suppose. What do you have in mind?" he asked.

"Why don't you come to my house for supper tonight? Faye wants me to cook for the boarders, and I'd love for you to join us. After dinner, we could stroll through the garden and talk, or head to the parlor for some games."

"Well, seeing that I'm waiting for Ezra to get my horse shod—I'm not sure how long that will take."

"That's perfect then," she said with a smile. "If you can be there before six, we'll eat right afterwards."

"Sounds great," Hardin replied, watching Lydia get up from her chair, her gaze still locked on him.

"I haven't seen you in a while, Hardin," she said, "and I'm really glad you're coming."

"Yes, me too, Lydia," Hardin responded as she turned and walked toward a customer's table.

Hardin was still trying to understand how Lydia's mood had changed so drastically in such a short period. Just days earlier, she had been furious and refused to speak to him. What could have caused this sudden eagerness to reconnect?

He looked up and saw Darcy approaching with his breakfast. She set it on the table, then said, "I noticed Lydia and you talking again."

"Yes, and I'm curious why she suddenly wants to be friends," Hardin replied.

"I can tell you exactly why," Darcy said, a smile playing at the corners of her lips. She knew all too well the games Lydia sometimes played with men. "Lydia heard about your dinner with the new doctor, Victoria Hawkins. She's jealous—that's all there is to it."

"Interesting," Hardin mused. "Just a few days ago, I thought she couldn't stand me."

"Marshal, Lydia doesn't know what she wants. I should probably tell you that she's been writing to a man she knew from long ago, trying to lure him to Bitterroot Springs."

"Then I wonder what she wants from me."

"Well, she's a woman. Most of us are simply looking for a man who can offer us a better life than what we can hope to find in these cattle and mining towns."

"I can imagine how difficult that is, Darcy."

"You'd better eat your food before it gets cold," Darcy said, gazing back toward the kitchen. "I need to get back."

As Hardin savored his meal, Lydia passed by several times, flashing him a smile. Once he finished, he paid for his meal and headed out to check on his horse.

The afternoon had dragged on slowly as Lydia prepared the evening meal. As she finished, she set a bowl of mashed potatoes on the table, glancing at the front door and hoping Hardin hadn't changed his mind. After hearing that the new doctor was interested in him, she thought that some romantic persuasion might help to salvage their relationship, especially since she had muddled things up a few days ago.

She saw Faye marching toward the front door, and soon after, Hardin stepped inside. A pang of anxiety surged through her as she left the dining area and fetched the last two bowls of food, placing them on the table.

Faye stepped into the dining room. "Are you ready for everyone, dear?" she asked.

"Yes, please have them take their seats while I grab some glasses," Lydia replied.

As Faye guided everyone to the table, Lydia quickly returned with the glasses, set them down, and took a seat next to Hardin. "Marshal, would you bless the meal?" It was a hopeful assumption that Hardin could say a prayer, but something about him hinted that beneath his rugged exterior lay a religious man.

"Sure, if you'll all bow your heads," Hardin replied. "Father in Heaven, we are truly thankful for your benefits. We ask that you bless this food to our bodies and those who have prepared it. Amen."

"A lovely prayer," Faye said. "Now, Lydia, start passing the food around to our newest guest. He's a hardworking man who could use plenty of nourishment."

Hardin took the bowl of mashed potatoes from Lydia, scooping out a generous portion before passing it to the man in the suit and tie sitting next to him. "I don't believe we've met." The man smiled modestly as he replied, "Virgil Creed is my name."

"Oh, pardon my forgetfulness," Faye interjected. "I should have introduced you all to the marshal. The gentleman sitting across from you, Marshal, is Mr. Rufus Taggart. The lady at the other end is my dear friend, Vera Watts. You've met Virgil and Lydia already."

"I'm pleased to meet all of you," Hardin responded.

Before long, everyone had filled their plates and settled into their meals, the atmosphere resonating with the sounds of cheerful conversation.

"Marshal Hardin, I heard talk of rustlers in the area," Virgil said. "One man mentioned that his ranch lost fifteen head of cattle just a few nights ago. How do you go about catching men like that?"

"Apprehending rustlers who cut herds or rebrand cattle is complicated. They move around a lot. The last group I caught—a cowboy working for a ranch—showed me where they were rebranding. We set a trap and arrested them. Unfortunately, I don't have any leads right now, though a simple tip could change that."

"Where do all the cattle from the ranches end up?" Vera Watts inquired.

Hardin finished chewing his bite and replied, "Some of them stay right here to feed people, while the others are taken to the stockyards and later herded to a steamboat. I've heard that the railroad will soon open up shipments from Miles City, and once that happens, the ranchers will be able to ship them faster."

Vera listened attentively to Hardin's words and replied, "That sounds like quite a lot of work."

Hardin nodded toward her. "Wrangling cattle is hard work, ma'am, but for some men, it's all they know."

After they finished eating, Faye and Rufus Taggart began discussing newspaper articles from back East. Lydia motioned for Hardin to follow her.

"Faye, I'll be back in a while to help with the dishes," Lydia said. "I'd like to show the marshal your flower garden."

"Don't worry about the dishes, dear. Vera and I will take care of them," Faye assured her.

"Thank you very much," Lydia said with a smile as she stood from her chair and led Hardin through a hallway and out the back door.

They reached a walkway leading to a charming pergola, its white painted structure adorned with flowering vines cascading over the top and down the sides. An inviting bench sat in the center.

"This is very nice," Hardin remarked. "I didn't know this was here."

"Faye had to show me; otherwise, I would never have found it either," Lydia replied with a smile.

As they settled onto the bench, Hardin couldn't shake a wave of apprehension. He genuinely liked Lydia, but he couldn't forget her frustration over the missed buggy ride and picnic, or her disappointment in his work. Then there was Victoria Hawkins, for whom he felt a growing attraction. At least the doctor understood the importance of his job and knew he would need to be away from time to time.

Lydia reached out to him, wrapping her arms around his neck. She looked into Hardin's brown eyes, then pressed her lips softly against his.

Hardin kissed her back but felt a pressing need to explain how he felt. "Lydia, I'm sorry. I really like you, but it seems that whenever we get close, something deep inside me raises a barrier."

Lydia's smile faded as she stood, turning her gaze toward the flowers in the garden.

Hardin rose and moved close behind her. "What I'm trying to say is that my physical being is eager to pursue a relationship with you, but my heart is reluctant and tells me I shouldn't."

Lydia spun around to face him, a fragile smile on her face. Hardin could see that his words had wounded her. "So, I was right about you the first time. You're just another lawman married to your work, who has no time for a woman."

"Lydia, it's not like that at all," Hardin replied earnestly. "From the first day I met you at the café, I felt a desire to get to know you."

"Then why don't you?" Lydia challenged, her voice trembling. "I'm right here, Marshal."

Hardin had no answer, and he truly cared for Lydia, but the demands of his job felt like an insurmountable barrier. He worried that things would never change.

Lydia turned and walked quickly toward the house. Just before she reached the door, she whirled back around to face him. "I want you to leave. Don't talk to anyone—just go!" With that, she turned again and went inside, the door shutting behind her.

Hardin exhaled softly, placed his hat firmly on his head, and followed her through the door. After gently closing it behind him, he stepped out the front entrance without saying a word.

23

The night unleashed heavy thunderstorms, with lightning flashing across the sky and several inches of relentless rain turning Main Street at Bitterroot Springs into a muddy quagmire. When morning came, Hardin slipped on his rain slicker and made his way to the café.

While enjoying breakfast, he received a telegram from William Boyd. The message said that an outlaw named Ted Bond, along with an accomplice, had escaped from a marshal during his transfer from Kansas to Miles City, Montana, for trial. Hardin knew the telegram was not merely a report of the outlaw's escape—it was, in fact, a special assignment. Fortunately, the storms had eased into a light, steady rain.

After saddling Amos, he stopped at the general store for supplies, where he ran into Colt Jackson from the Moore Ranch. Upon learning about Hardin's pursuit of two fugitives riding together, Jackson insisted on joining the search. Once he had gathered supplies, Hardin rode to a place to meet Jackson, who had left to unload a wagon. After a long wait, he spotted a sorrel horse and its rider approaching.

"I wondered if they'd let you leave," Hardin said.

"Oh, the boss didn't mind," Jackson replied. "He said men like you're after need to be behind bars."

"He's right."

As they turned to ride away, Jackson asked, "Marshal, are you sure about going after them? If they came from Kansas, we might never pick up their tracks, especially after this rain."

Hardin nodded. "All I know for sure is, they headed toward the Big Bottom area without supplies. They'll have to buy some food and supplies or steal it from someone."

"Then this is going to be interesting," Jackson said with a grin.

By the time they reached the halfway point to Miles City, the rain had finally stopped. Hardin quickly unrolled a canvas and set up a tent, just in case more rain rolled in during the night.

"Maybe this will keep us dry if the rain starts again," Hardin declared.

Jackson grabbed the horse's reins. "I'll water our horses while you get that sorted."

Once settled beneath the canvas, they shared some beef jerky and coffee before lying down for an early night's rest.

As the sun broke over the treetops at daybreak, they gathered their supplies, saddled their horses, and hit the trail.

"So you knew James Moore already?" Jackson asked.

"Yeah, we rode the Pony Express together in our younger days," Hardin replied.

"I heard that the men who rode the Pony Express were fearless, mostly riding through Indian lands."

"We did, but we always kept the fastest mounts for those territories," Hardin recalled.

As they reached Miles City, Hardin brought their horses to a halt outside the general store. "Let's check if Bond and his partner made it here for supplies," he suggested.

Sheriff Shepard walked their way as they dismounted. "Hello, Marshal. Are those supplies telling me you're heading out of town?" he asked.

"Yep," Hardin responded. "I'm tracking an escaped prisoner who was spotted riding this way with another man."

"Oh, yeah, I got a telegram saying to be on the lookout for them," Shepard said. "The main one, Ted Bond, is a dangerous scoundrel."

"Do you know anything about this other fellow riding with him?" Hardin asked.

Shepard thought for a moment. "Yeah, he goes by the name of Hawk Blackthorn. Half Apache and reportedly as ruthless as Bond. I heard they kicked him out of his tribe after he cut up two people. So, what brought you to Miles City? Did you think they were here?"

"I figured they'd stop for supplies if they made it this far."

"They're not in Miles City, or I would know," Shepard said.

Hardin grimaced. "That means they'll probably target a settler's camp or a homestead along the trail. I expect we'll find some bodies."

"I wouldn't be surprised," Shepard acknowledged.

"Well, Sheriff, we'd better head out. Want to find some signs of them before dark," Hardin said as he mounted Amos.

"Good luck to you. Better keep your eyes peeled—they're both killers."

Hardin nodded and turned his horse east with Colt Jackson riding alongside him.

After several hours of riding, they reached a fork in the trail. The right path was the one Hardin had taken when he first rode to Miles City, while the left led into the rugged Big Bottom country—a region known only as wilderness, and a place where the Indians who fled the reservation sought refuge.

Hardin brought Amos to a stop, studying the two trails. "We've got to go north, and it will take us through some dangerous territory. We might run into Indians before we find Bond's trail."

"Is there any other way they could have rode?" Jackson asked.

"I don't believe so. The telegram said the marshal tracked Bond to the Big Bottom area after his escape. The older marshal wouldn't take the posse in, and I guess I was the closest one available," Hardin explained.

"Marshal, maybe you should've told them no."

"I wouldn't last long as a marshal if I started shirking assignments."

"But, from what we know about these men, you might live longer by turning it down," Jackson said.

Hardin grinned and glanced at him as they rode along. "We'll ride slower to avoid any unnecessary trouble."

Jackson chucked. "That's mighty comforting, Marshal."

A few miles further down the trail, Hardin peered ahead intently. "I see a creek up ahead. Let's stop and make camp for the night."

Jackson gave a nod. "Good. I'd better gather plenty of dry wood—it feels like snow is coming."

After unsaddling the horses, Hardin led them to the water while Jackson went in search of wood to start the fire.

Hardin soon returned with the horses and tied them up to a nearby tree. "I wouldn't be surprised if there are wolves in these woods."

Jackson took a glance toward the woods. "Yeah, maybe even bears, I guess. And we might wish we had one of those bear skins tonight."

"You're not worried about getting cold, are you?" Hardin asked.

Jackson shrugged, tilting his head. "Marshal, let's just say, I can handle the hot weather better than the cold."

Hardin grinned. "As long as we keep the fire going and some hot coffee in us, I think we'll be just fine."

An hour later, the campfire blazed with a bed of coals as they leaned back against their saddles.

"Are you a religious man, Marshal Hardin?" Jackson asked.

"I'd like to think so," Hardin replied. "Though I'm no preacher, if that's what you mean? Why do you ask?"

"I've been in some dangerous situations in my life, especially around cattle. Got to wonder what happens after we die. Do you think there's a Heaven?" Jackson inquired.

Hardin took a sip of coffee and replied, "I do—the Bible says so."

"Bible," Jackson mumbled, taking a moment to ponder his reply. "But what about killing? I heard you took down a gunhand a few days ago. Doesn't the Bible teach that's wrong?"

Hardin looked at him earnestly. "I once heard a preacher explain it. He said there's a difference between murder and self-defense—one is wrong, and the other is justifiable. You should never go into a fight intending to take a life, but sometimes you have to protect yourself and others from those who mean harm."

Jackson silently reflected on Hardin's response as he pulled a blanket over himself and drifted off to sleep.

24

The morning dawned with a light dusting of snow, bringing a quiet hush over the landscape as Hardin and Jackson departed from camp. They followed the northwest trail for miles, seeing no horses or wagons until two trappers appeared walking on the horizon.

As the trappers drew within twenty feet, one suddenly raised a shotgun and fired, narrowly missing Hardin. The marshal drew his revolver and returned fire, hitting the man in the leg. The two men ran into the woods as Hardin and Jackson dismounted and quickly sought cover behind a pair of large oak trees.

"What do they want with us?" Jackson asked, glancing nervously toward the woods.

"I figure they want our horses," Hardin replied, "and maybe our supplies too."

"They can't have them," Jackson declared firmly.

"You reckon, but we may have to fight to get out of this," Hardin cautioned.

Jackson's eyes widened with concern. "Those escaped outlaws could slip out of the territory while we're stuck here."

"What do you suggest?" Hardin asked, turning to face him.

Jackson pointed to his badge. "Tell them you're a marshal."

"I can try, but it may not matter. Hey, you trappers! I'm the U.S. Marshal for the Montana Territory, and we don't want any trouble. We're looking for a couple of outlaws who might have rode this way. We need to get down this trail."

"Ain't seen them," one of the trappers called out. "We ain't leaving without your horses, Marshal."

"I've got to have my horses—we still have a long way to go," Hardin insisted.

"Yeah, well, we need them too," the other trapper responded.

"Are they worth dying over?" Hardin asserted. "One of you is already bleeding from my bullet."

"Just a scrape," the trapper said.

"He's alright, Marshal," the first trapper shouted. "Maybe you should think about who might die here. Our scatter guns have you pinned down!"

"They aren't giving up easily," Hardin muttered.

Jackson glanced warily at the woods behind them, weighing their options. "Marshal, I think I can slip through the woods behind us and get around to the other side. That might give me a better angle to shoot from."

Hardin pondered Jackson's idea for a moment. "Alright. Once you're in position, lay down some rounds so I can advance. And whatever you do, don't shoot me."

The young cowboy nodded, then turned and crept quietly through the brush. Hardin caught a glimpse of him changing directions before he vanished into the foliage. A few moments later, the sharp crack of rifle fire shattered the silence, drawing the trappers' attention toward Jackson. Several rounds of shot-gun blasts echoed through the air as the two men fired back in response.

Seizing the opportunity, Hardin crouched low, dashed across the trail, and maneuvered behind the two men.

"Hold your fire!" Hardin ordered, emerging from cover with his gun trained on them. "Drop those weapons on the ground. Jackson, get our horses over here!"

As he waited, he examined the two trappers closely, noting their fur hats and rugged clothing pieced together from animal skins. Large skinning knives hung from their belts, with bundles of dried furs strapped to their backs. Hesitation flickered in their eyes as they gripped their weapons, weighing Hardin's command.

"Put 'em down and leave them there," Hardin ordered sternly.

"Aw, we gotta have our weapons, Marshal," the first trapper grumbled. "We might run into bears or a lion."

"Then stop trying to steal horses," Hardin retorted, his voice sharp. "If you want some to ride, go buy a couple."

"We don't want 'em for riding. Me and Hoge need 'em to haul our furs to the trading post," the other man insisted gruffly.

Hardin turned to him. "You're Hoge Finnegan?" he inquired.

"That's right," the trapper replied.

"Someone was asking about you at Miles City—a woman," Hardin said.

"Harriet, my sister, I reckon. Don't fret about her. I'll stop by after we head to the trading post."

Hardin shifted his gaze to the other man. "What's *your* name, mister?"

"Levi Hawthorne. What cho gonna do with us, Marshal?"

"I ought to drag you *both* to Miles City and lock you up for attempted horse theft, but I'm not going to do that," Hardin replied calmly.

"You're not?" Hawthorne asked, his eyes wide with surprise.

"I won't this time, but if I hear of you stealing horses, I'll track you down and bring you both in," Hardin warned, his voice carrying a firm edge.

"We won't do it again, Marshal," Finnegan replied with a regretful tone. "It was a fool notion, but we figured we'd have some fun."

"Fun? I'll find my pleasure locking you two up!" Hardin answered, sounding agitated. Noticing that Jackson had gathered their horses and was waiting along the trail, he turned again to the trappers and said, "Leave those weapons on the ground until we're out of sight."

"Sure thing, we're in no hurry," Finnegan replied.

With that, Hardin walked toward his horse, mounted up, and he and Jackson rode away.

25

The trail grew increasingly difficult to navigate as the snowfall continued, but soon, they caught the scent of smoke drifting in from the north.

"Keep an eye out for a campfire through the trees," Hardin instructed. "We mustn't let them know how close we are." With the trees having shed their leaves, the bare branches offered a clearer view of the forest. They slowed their pace, carefully scanning for any signs of movement.

"There, Marshal! Smoke," Jackson said, gesturing eastward. "It looks like a cabin back that way."

"I see it too," Hardin replied. "Let's dismount here." They tied their horses, grabbed their rifles, and strolled toward the cabin with caution, positioning themselves behind some trees.

"It won't be easy to flesh them out," Jackson noted.

"Agreed. Let's think this through for a moment," Hardin said, surveying the area.

"Marshal, they gotta have their horses stashed nearby. Surely we can find them."

"Likely in a shelter behind the cabin," Hardin speculated. "I'll circle to the rear and find a spot to shoot from. Give me about ten minutes, then call them out. Tell them to come out with their hands up, or we're coming in."

"They might try sneaking out the back," Jackson warned.

Hardin nodded as he turned to leave. "Let them. If you hear gunfire, come running."

Slipping from his cover, Hardin crept slowly through the deepening snow, taking a wide berth around the cabin. Once at the back, he spotted a shed covered in snow with two horses inside. The shed stood about thirty feet from the back door, forcing anyone inside to trudge through the snow to reach it.

A few moments later, Jackson's voice echoed through the cold air: "Ted Bond and Hawk Blackthorn! This is Marshal Reuben Hardin, and I've got a posse with me. There's no need to resist—come out with your hands up, or we'll come in!"

Faint voices stirred inside the cabin, confirming the outlaws' presence.

"Hey, Marshal. This is Bond. We'd rather stay warm inside, thanks," came the reply from within.

"We've got you surrounded!" Jackson shouted back. "You don't come out, we'll smoke you out."

"Come on, lawman. Can't you wait till it warms up?" Bond taunted. "Or join us by the fire before you freeze to death out there!"

Laughter echoed inside the cabin.

Hardin shook his head, believing it would take some effort to get them out.

"We've come a long way for you," Jackson called out, "and we're not backing down!"

Minutes ticked by without a reply until Hardin, crouched behind a stack of firewood, spotted the back door creak open, and someone's head poked out to scout the back. Two men suddenly burst out the door, carrying saddlebags and rifles, sprinting through the snow toward their horses. Hardin quickly raised his rifle and fired at the first one, but the shot went wide.

They reached the shed, where Bond hurriedly began saddling their horses as Hawk returned fire, his shot splintering the stack of firewood near Hardin. Hardin fired two rounds, but the Apache agilely ducked inside the corner of the shed.

A sudden burst of light illuminated the shed's interior as Bond flung open a second door on the back of the shed and urged his mount out into the snow.

The outlaw's horse floundered in the heavy drifts, buying Hardin seconds to get off a few more rounds. One bullet found its mark, striking Bond in the left side and piercing his lung, sending him tumbling to the ground.

Seeing Bond go down, Hawk mounted his horse and kicked him into the storm. As the horse bolted forward, Jackson fired a round, grazing Hawk's arm. In retaliation, Hawk steadied his aim and shot back, hitting Jackson in the side and causing him to stagger.

By then, Hardin had closed in on the shed. He aimed and fired, the bullet striking Hawk in the upper back. The Apache slumped from his horse and collapsed into the snow.

Hardin rushed over, kneeling beside the man, and turned him over. "Hawk, who was in the cabin when you came here?"

The Apache looked up at him, his face twisted in agony, and a faint, defiant grin crossed his lips. "Two old f... fur trappers," he gasped. "Bond killed them."

"Where are they?"

"Bond took them t... to woods for wolves," Hawk whispered, with a shallow breath, his voice fading as his eyes fluttered shut.

Shifting his focus, Hardin dashed across the snow to Jackson, who lay slumped on the ground, clutching his side. "How's it going, cowboy?"

"Could be better," Jackson replied through gritted teeth. "I should have stayed behind cover."

"Where're you hit?"

"Right side," he winced.

"I'm getting you to Miles City to a doctor," Hardin said firmly. "First, I need to get you inside and dress that wound. Think you can walk, Jackson?"

"I'll try, Marshal," Jackson replied, his face contorted with pain.

With Hardin's steady support, Jackson slowly rose, leaning against him as they trudged through the snow toward the back door. Once inside, Hardin spotted a bed in the corner and carefully guided Jackson over to it.

"I'll find something to staunch the bleeding," Hardin assured him. "Keep pressure on the wound."

"Ow, that hurts something fierce," Jackson gasped, wincing as he pressed his hand against the injury.

After quickly rummaging through a cabinet, Hardin pulled out several rags. "I found some things we can use." He tore one rag into strips and used another to fashion a makeshift bandage, wrapping it securely around Jackson's wound. "Hopefully, this holds until we get you to town," he said with a nod.

A dreadful thought raced through Hardin's mind as he gazed down at Jackson's pale face. If they left now, they'd have to battle the snow and difficult trail, but staying at the cabin meant no doctor and the risk of Jackson's condition worsening. He knew they couldn't afford to wait any longer as time was slipping away.

Jackson lay on the bed, his eyes closed, having fallen into a state of unconsciousness. Hardin had managed to stop the bleeding, but this was only a temporary fix—Jackson needed proper medical attention soon, or it could be too late.

Determined, Hardin scanned the cabin for any supplies that might aid the journey. He grabbed a few extra rags and two thick blankets, then hurried outside to get the horses. With Jackson's horse secured near the back door, Hardin wrapped one blanket around the cowboy, carefully lifted him onto the saddle, and tied him in place. He then mounted Amos and led the way, pushing into the unforgiving storm.

After two grueling days and one frigid night on the trail, Hardin finally reached Miles City with Jackson. Sheriff Shepard directed him to Solomon Burke, the town's doctor, on the main street.

Dr. Burke examined Jackson as he lay on the examination table, his face expressing concern. "The hole in his back wasn't caused by the bullet exiting," the doctor observed, carefully probing the wound.

"Then what caused it, Doctor?" Hardin inquired.

"I'll know when I get inside, but I suspect the bullet lodged near his ribs and possibly chipped off a piece of bone," Burke explained.

Hardin's brows furrowed as he looked down at his wounded friend. "Will he be alright?"

"If he hasn't lost too much blood, there's still hope," Dr. Burke replied. "It's remarkable you managed to bring him here alive through that brutal snowstorm and all the way from Big Bottom. Leave him with me for now—you can return in a few hours."

"Thank you, Doctor," Hardin replied, somewhat relieved. "I might take a moment to rest myself."

"That's fine. Just knock when you return."

After leaving the doctor's office, Hardin led the horses through the snow–covered streets to the livery stable, where he settled them in. The weight of the past days pressed heavily on him as he made his way to the hotel.

Once inside, he headed up the stairs, removed his gun belt, and hung it on the headboard. Collapsing onto the bed, the exhaustion from the grueling journey finally overtook him; his muscles ached, and his mind, fraught with worry for Jackson, finally surrendered to a sleep.

26

After meeting with Dr. Burke the next morning and confirming Colt Jackson would recover, Hardin left word with Sheriff Shepard to inform James Moore about his man before departing. Although wagons had packed down the snow, the biting cold and relentless wind made the journey a grueling ordeal.

As he reached the midpoint to Bitterroot Springs, he came to a hill that offered much-needed break from the harsh wind for both himself and Amos. He quickly gathered some dry branches and started a small fire to ward off the chill and brew a pot of coffee. Knowing the weather might only worsen, he quickly drank a cup before moving on.

An hour after nightfall, Hardin rode into the mostly deserted town of Bitterroot Springs. He opened the door to the livery stable, and Ezra

Tate soon emerged from a back room, bundled in a heavy coat.

"Hey, Ezra," Hardin said, his breath fogging in the frigid air as he stepped inside.

"I can't believe you're out in this weather," Ezra replied, shaking his head. "This kind of cold will make a man sick for sure."

"Yeah, I know," Hardin admitted, rubbing his hands together for warmth. "Could you give Amos a little extra grain tonight? It's been a rough few days for him."

"Yes, sir, I will," Ezra assured him.

"I noticed several wagon tracks on my way in, but the town seems awful quiet tonight," Hardin remarked.

Ezra furrowed his brow as he reached for the horses' reins. "I did see Grover French earlier when he was unloading supplies at the mercantile. Any other tracks likely belong to ranchers picking up grain and supplies. This cold is tough on the animals."

"I wonder if the café is still open," Hardin mused, his voice echoing in the quiet space.

"Oh, yeah," Ezra nodded, shoving his hands deeper into his coat pockets. "The café's pretty much the only spot you'll find open in this weather."

"Thanks, I can use some food," Hardin said, stepping outside into the biting wind.

He trudged through the snow to the café and pushed open the door. Inside, a few hardy customers huddled against the chill to grab a quick meal. Spotting Grover French sitting alone at a corner table, Hardin approached. "Mind if I join you?"

"Not at all. Please, sit down, Marshal," French said, gesturing to the empty chair.

Hardin sat down on the other side. "How do you manage to get around in weather like this?"

"I don't much," French replied with a shrug. "These Montana winters make it darn near impossible for a man to earn a living, so I stock up during the best seasons to tide me over. Those steamboats quit running the moment the ice starts forming—those captains aren't about to risk getting trap like they did in '69."

"So, the supplies get offloaded and have to last everyone through the winter," Hardin deduced, piecing it together.

"You got it," French confirmed with a nod.

Lydia set a plate of food in front of Grover French. "Is there anything else you need, Mr. French?"

"Not for me, but I reckon this Marshal is hungry," French replied, glancing at Hardin with a smile.

Hardin caught Lydia's fleeting glance, noting her discomfort as she avoided his eyes. "I'll have whatever the special is today, along with some coffee," he said.

"Of course," Lydia replied with a quick nod, then turned and headed back to the kitchen.

French leaned in toward the table. "I couldn't help but notice she was avoiding eye contact with you, Marshal. Have I missed something?"

Hardin shifted in his seat, choosing his words carefully. "Lydia has feelings for me, but my frequent absences don't align with her idea of a relationship," he explained.

"Seems to me all the women I've ever known can be quite selfish," French remarked, shaking his head with a wry smile.

"Let's hope they're not that way," Hardin replied with a hint of optimism.

Lydia returned, carefully placing Hardin's plate and a cup of black coffee in front of him. She stood with her hands on her hips and asked, "Is there anything else you need, Marshal?"

"This will be just fine, thank you." Hardin met Lydia's gaze as she turned and walked away.

French caught her quick exit before turning his gaze back to Hardin. "I do think she's angry with you."

Hardin paused to chew a bite of his food, then set his fork down. "We were good friends until she expected me to abandon work for her," he said, his voice steady but laced with resignation. "I feel for the man who tries to fit into her self-centered view of relationships."

The two men finished their meal in relative silence and sat drinking their coffee when a young man about thirty years old burst through the café door. His face flushed and urgent, he scanned the room and hurried straight to their table. "Marshal, there's a man down in the alley next to the saloon. My friend rode to get Dr. Hawkins—he's in a really bad way."

Hardin quickly donned his coat and hat. "Mr. French, I'd better look into this. Lead the way, son." After tossing some coins on the table to cover his meal, he followed the young man out the door and down the dimly lit street toward the saloon. The alley beside the establishment was convenient for unloading supplies, but it was notorious for being a hotspot for criminal activity.

Several men had gathered around the man lying on the cold, snowy ground, their breaths visible in the frigid air as they hovered.

Hardin quickly assessed the situation and noticed a side door to the saloon. "One of you, check if that door is unlocked," he instructed firmly. "If it's not, go around and unlock it."

An older man with a thick beard stepped forward and pulled the door handle, discovering it was indeed unlocked. Hardin glanced at the group and nodded. "Alright, let's get him off the ground and inside out of the cold—carefully now."

They lifted the injured man and carried him through the door, gently laying him on the floor just as Dr. Hawkins arrived on her horse, accompanied by the cowboy who had alerted her. Victoria met Hardin's eyes with a friendly, reassuring glance. "How long has he been down?" she asked.

"Joe found him outside about half an hour ago when he was leaving the saloon," one of the cowboys explained, his pupils dilated from whiskey. "He thought he saw something suspicious in the alley."

"What's this man's name?" Dr. Hawkins inquired as she kneeled beside him to examine his injury.

"That's Caleb Driscoll," the cowboy replied. "He's one of the lumbermen. I saw him playing cards earlier, and he won a lot of money."

Dr. Hawkins gently rolled him onto his side as she examined him thoroughly. Blood pooled on the wooden floor, exposing a severe wound on the back of his head that sent a chill through the room. "It looks like someone struck him with a blunt object," she assessed, her voice calm but grave. "His skull is fractured—pretty badly."

Hardin turned to the cowboy. "What's your name?"

"I'm Darren Marks," the cowboy replied.

"Do you know the names of the others in the card game?" Hardin pressed.

"No, sir, but I'm sure they were from the timber company," Darren answered. "They all looked rough—unshaven and had on those plaid shirts like they wear."

Hardin shifted his attention back to the victim. "Hopefully, he'll regain consciousness and tell us who did this."

Dr. Hawkins shook her head slowly. "I'm afraid not—he just passed. The blow to his head was far too severe." She stood up, wiping her hands on a cloth. "Now you've got a murder on your hands, Marshal."

"And a robbery," Darren added.

"Unless his friends know who might have done this," Hardin said, kneeling beside the deceased, "we may never find the person."

He searched through the man's coat and britches pockets. "Yeah, looks like whoever did this got his money," he said, glancing at Victoria, with a nod. "I suppose you're done here."

"Yes—I've got to get out of this wind," Dr. Hawkins replied, pulling her coat tighter around her as she prepared to leave.

"Will you be okay riding home?" Hardin asked.

"Yes, I'll be fine, Marshal," she assured him, offering a quick smile before stepping out into the cold.

As some of the men began carefully gathering the body to transport it to the undertaker, Hardin shifted his focus to the evening stagecoach rumbling into town. Three passengers disembarked and made their way toward the lights of the café. Lydia stood on the boardwalk, waiting for a man in a dark overcoat and a matching bowler hat. She guided him across the street and helped him load his baggage into the back of a buggy hitched to a horse.

Lydia spotted Hardin watching them and gave a slight smirk as she gently swayed her shoulders, getting into the buggy and driving away.

Hardin watched them leave, wondering if this was the man Darcy had spoken of. He figured she must have invited him to Bitterroot Springs after he'd turned her down, perhaps to stir up some jealousy. It was for the best, he told himself, a wave of relief coming over him as he accepted that this chapter of his life had finally closed.

Redirecting his attention to the pressing matter at hand, he resolved to ride out to the timber cutter's camp the next day. He hoped someone there might know the men from the card game or provide him with a clue to clear up the mystery surrounding the man's death in the alley.

27

Hardin stood quietly, observing the carpenters as they hammered away on the jail's framework. The stage driver, Zeb Carver, made his way over to him. "Marshal, I've only just started with the stage line, but I learned why the previous driver quit."

"I don't know what you're talking about," Hardin replied. "Explain it to me."

"My man who rides shotgun, Thaddeus Boone, tells me Indians attempted to ambush the stage twice now."

"What exactly are they after?" Hardin asked, a line etching between his brows.

"From what he's told me, they're mostly after horses or food," Zeb explained. "I'd appreciate it if you'd come by the stage line office and help me persuade the owner to hire extra guards for protection."

"I doubt he'll take me seriously based only on what you've shared," Hardin replied.

Undeterred, Zeb pressed on, "Would you at least consider riding along with us to Miles City, just in case they strike again?"

Hardin paused for a moment, weighing Zeb's request against his other responsibilities. He knew he had other duties in the territory and shouldn't spare any time to escort the stage. "Look, mister, I can't afford to spend two or three days working security for the stage line," he said firmly.

"Marshal, I've got six passengers on board—three are women. Do you really want to risk them getting hurt?" Zeb implored.

Hardin was all too aware that trouble could erupt anywhere in this wild land, but the trail to Miles City was notorious for ambushes. "I'll speak with the owner, but no promises."

Together, they walked to the stage line office. Inside, a tall man with a thick mustache, dressed in earthy brown britches and a faded orange shirt, sat behind a worn desk. As they approached, he rose slowly, his expression guarded, and waited for them.

"What is it now, Zeb?" the stage owner asked.

"Same as before—more guns to go along with us, sir," Zeb said. "I brought this marshal in here, and he would like to speak to you."

"Marshal, glad you stopped by," Jedediah Colter replied, his voice cordial yet dismissive. "But I don't think this is any of your concern."

"Maybe not," Hardin said, crossing his arms as he met Colter's gaze, "unless the Indians are causing trouble along the route. Lawfully, I can require you to provide the stage driver with some additional help before anyone gets hurt. Or, you could reach out to the army for help."

"Bah, the army won't lift a finger unless they know exactly where the Indians plan to strike," Colter responded with a confident wave of his hand. "My men have already fended off those renegades twice without issue. The man riding shotgun is more than capable."

"Regardless," Hardin countered, "I plan to ride along to Miles City to get a better sense of the situation myself. If the Indians show up and pose a threat, I'll strongly advise you to increase protection for your passengers."

"Now, hold on a minute," Colter argued, his voice rising as he leaned forward over the desk, "I can't turn a profit if I'm pouring all my earnings into protection. I'm already doing what I can within my budget."

"Well, you may need to do more," Hardin replied firmly. "When lives are at risk, I have the authority to shut down your operation."

Colter stared at him, shocked that the marshal might go that far. "Well, Marshal, perhaps we can reach an understanding," Colter suggested, a sly edge creeping into his voice as he motioned for Hardin to approach the desk. He slipped open a drawer and pulled out twenty dollars. "Maybe this will help you see things my way."

Hardin met Colter's gaze with a steely stare, his jaw tightening. "I can't believe you'd bribe a U.S. marshal," he said.

"Don't you want it?" Colter pressed, desperation flickering in his eyes.

"Put that back in your drawer, Mr. Colter," Hardin warned, "before I take you in. The new jail's coming along well enough that I could lock you in one of the cells. When I return, we can discuss this matter further." With that, Hardin turned on his heel and strode toward the door, Zeb trailing quietly behind him.

Stepping outside, the bustle of passengers already boarding the stagecoach greeted them. Thaddeus Boone was perched above on his knees, busy loading cargo onto the stagecoach. "Are we ready to leave?" he called out.

"In a few minutes," Zeb responded, glancing at the growing crowd. "Marshal, I can't wait for you—we're on a schedule."

"Go ahead," Hardin assured him with a nod. "I'll get my horse and gear from the livery and catch up with you on the trail."

"Alrighty, thank you."

"Don't thank me just yet," Hardin remarked with a wry smile. "I haven't seen any Indians."

A few miles down the trail, Thaddeus glanced over his shoulder to find Marshal Hardin. "Don't see that lawman yet," he said, shielding his eyes from the glaring sun. "Do you reckon he's changed his mind?"

"Don't start me lying—I don't know much about the man," Zeb replied.

"We're not far from where we came across that band of Indians," Thaddeus noted.

"Just keep that rifle handy," Zeb instructed. "I warned the men riding the stage that if we spot Indians, they need to be ready to help out."

"Zeb, Taggert always said not to let the passengers use their weapons," Thaddeus countered. "He said it might draw bullets toward innocent people and cause more harm than good."

"Sounds like Taggert had some peculiar rules," Zeb replied. "I'm just trying to save lives."

Thaddeus peered again over the stacked cargo. "Hey, I see a rider coming up behind us. Might be the marshal."

"If that's him, he'll ride up beside us or close by," Zeb replied.

Moments later, Hardin rode up alongside the stagecoach and gave a quick wave. He followed along behind them for the next ten miles before Zeb eased back on the reins, gradually slowing the stagecoach to a halt near the river-bank.

"What are you stopping for?" Hardin asked, riding his horse alongside.

"Water the horses," Zeb answered, stepping down from the driver's seat. "There's a good spot here by the river to let them drink. I was pushing them pretty hard to make up time, so I figured I'd better tend to them before we press on."

"No problem," Hardin said as he dismounted and walked Amos toward the river.

Thaddeus knelt by the river and filled a bucket with water. "Marshal, Zeb's telling you the truth about those Indians," he said, hoisting out the bucket with a grunt. "I was riding shotgun twice when we ran into 'em."

"If they're looking for food," Hardin replied, "I have to wonder if the army is providing what they promised."

"I wouldn't know about that, but I figure this group has ridden away from the reservation," Thaddeus speculated.

"Yeah, you're probably right," Hardin said.

As Thaddeus turned to head back to the stagecoach, he hesitated, then pivoted on his heel. "Marshal, I heard someone say the Indians are gathering to prepare for a showdown with Colonel Custer and his men. Maybe these left the reservation to join in."

"That may be right," Hardin replied. "I'll speak to Colonel Miles when I get to the fort. Perhaps he can shed some light on the situation."

Zeb warned Hardin that the stagecoach would be moving at a fast pace for the remainder of the journey, which meant the passengers wouldn't see a proper meal until they reached town. Hardin knew from his Kansas travels that most stage lines had swing stations every ten to fifteen miles between home stations, but this rugged route stretched a grueling forty miles between water stops. He silently resolved that upon his return, he would insist that Jedediah Colter add at least one station between Bitterroot Springs and Miles City—not just to serve the weary passengers, but to tend to the horses properly.

As night began to fall, the stage finally rumbled into Miles City, kicking up a cloud of dust. Hardin led Amos to the livery stable, where he unsaddled and tended to his tired horse. Then, with his stomach growling from the long ride, he made his way to the hotel to secure a room before he ate. Entering the Cactus Blossom Hotel, he found the front counter unattended. However, the lively hum of conversation and the aroma of hearty meals drifted in from the adjacent dining room, where a crowd of townsfolk gathered for a meal.

"You came back," a familiar voice called from behind him. Hardin turned to find Abigail standing there, her beautiful face lit by a warm, welcoming smile.

"Abigail," he replied, a hint of amusement in his voice. "Did you miss me?"

"What makes you say that?" Abigail countered, raising an eyebrow with playful mischief.

"You were curious about my return," he teased.

Abigail nodded, presenting him with a saucy grin. "Oh, you've got it all wrong, Marshal. I figured you came back to visit one of our fine cathouses. Seems you've missed that opportunity."

"I'm still mulling that one over," Hardin responded, chuckling softly. "How about a room for the night?"

Abigail giggled before shifting her demeanor back to business. "What about one of the rooms you stayed in before? This one overlooks the town."

"That sounds perfect. What time does the restaurant close?" Hardin asked, glancing again toward the dining area.

"You have about thirty minutes," she replied, sliding the key across the counter.

He offered a polite nod, gathered his saddlebags from the counter, and turned toward the stairs. Once he reached his room, he unlocked the door, set down his saddlebags just inside the threshold, and then headed back downstairs.

Moments later, Hardin settled into a wooden chair at a dimly lit table in the dining room, as a young, dark-haired waitress approached with a tired but friendly smile. "We aren't cooking tonight, mister, but we still have some stew left and cornbread if you want it," she stated.

Hardin looked up at her with a smile. "How'd you know that's exactly what I wanted to order? And a glass of tea, please."

The waitress chuckled, then turned toward the kitchen, as Hardin's thoughts drifted back to Kansas. Hadn't he spent enough time in Montana and met Boyd's expectations? The people here were mostly friendly, yet something was missing—it didn't feel like home. Back in Kansas, the railroad hummed with activity, the cattle drives pulsed with life, and the people shared a camaraderie that put him at ease. Perhaps it was time to send a telegram to William Boyd and remind him.

The waitress returned promptly, placing a bowl of stew and a slice of cornbread on the table. "I'll get your tea right away, Marshal," she said, her eyes flicking to his badge with a spark of recognition before she hurried off again.

A moment later, she appeared with a glass of tea, setting it down beside his meal. "Do you need anything else?" she asked, wiping her hands on her apron.

"Only that I'd like to settle up so I can enjoy this and be on my way. How much do I owe you?" Hardin replied, reaching for his pocket.

She quoted the price with a nod, and Hardin paid her plus a tip. As she turned to walk away, she glanced back with a smile and added, "Thank you."

He returned the gesture with a courteous nod and dug into his meal, savoring the stew and the cornbread that still held a hint of warmth. Once he finished, he lingered at the table, sitting quietly as he gazed out the window. Someone had lit the street lamps, and they flickered to life against the deepening night. Most folks had retreated indoors, seeking shelter from the evening's biting chill, which even the hotel's wood-burning steam boiler couldn't fully ward off. To assist, they left extra blankets for the beds.

Hardin slowly stood, adjusting his hat with a weary hand. A warm bath sounded appealing, but he knew his need for rest outweighed his desire for cleanliness. As he made his way toward the stairs, his mind raced with all the tasks ahead: riding to the fort to speak with Colonel Miles, returning to Bitterroot Springs to insist that the stage owner add a station stop along the trail to Miles City, and taking a ride to the timber cutter's camp to learn more about the man who had died in the alley. He'd been on his way to the camp when the stage driver warned him about trouble with Indians on the trail to Miles City. With so much demanding his attention, he considered leaving now, but his body ached with exhaustion—he needed at least a few hours of sleep.

He pushed open the door to his room and went inside, collapsing onto the bed. Praying he could block out his racing thoughts and find some peace, he grabbed a blanket and pulled it over himself. As the warmth enveloped him, he soon drifted into a deep sleep.

28

Ezra Tate led a bay mare from the corral and secured her in a stall just as the main door creaked open. Two cowboys stepped inside, glancing around at the horses.

As Ezra emerged from the stall, he noticed them. "What can I do for you, fellows?" he asked.

One of the cowboys replied, "We're looking for the marshal."

"He's in the last stall, saddling his horse," Ezra said.

The cowboys made their way to the end, where they found Hardin cinching the saddle's girth. "Marshal Hardin, we caught one of them rustlers," one cowboy said.

Turning from Amos, Hardin walked toward them. "Where is he?" he asked.

The cowboy explained, "Our foreman, Tom Carson, has him tied on his horse just outside."

Hardin walked to the end of the hallway and stepped out of the building. Tom Carson and three of his men waited on their horses, alongside a man with his hands bound, clad in a heavy coat and a dark hat. Hardin approached, his eyes narrowing as he studied the man's face. "Is this the only one you saw?" he asked.

"Yes, sir, Marshal," Tom Carson confirmed. "One of my men spotted him at a campfire on the far side of Amos Cutler's ranch."

"That's nobody's land," the rustler protested.

"Everyone knows Cutler runs cattle on that land," Carson countered. "So, Marshal, what do you want us to do with him?"

Hardin paused for a moment, weighing his options, before replying, "Let's use him as bait."

"You'd have to hogtie him," Carson pointed out.

"Maybe not," Hardin said. "Let me get my horse." He led Amos out of the stable and swung into the saddle, gesturing for the others to follow and bring the rustler. Turning to the suspect, he said, "You'll be the first guest in the new Bitterroot Springs jail."

They brought their horses to a halt in front of the new jail and dismounted. One of Tom's men escorted the rustler inside, securing him in a cell as Hardin instructed.

"You can't leave me in here—it's freezing!" the rustler complained.

Hardin grinned. "This is an upgrade to that snow-covered ground you're used to," he said and hurried back to his horse.

As he mounted up, Tom Carson asked, "So what's this plan of yours?"

"We'll take his horse with us, and I'll show you," Hardin said. "First, I need to inform the mayor about our new prisoner."

After briefing the mayor on the situation, Hardin rejoined Carson and his men, heading back toward Amos Cutler's ranch. As they neared the spot where they'd captured the rustler, they stopped, wary of leaving tracks in the snow.

"You can tell me now, Marshal?" Carson asked.

"Yeah, have a couple of your men head in and build a strong fire at the camp," Hardin instructed calmly. "Then, use some brush or rocks to prop up his blanket and make it look like he's sleeping next to the fire. Tie the rustler's horse nearby to sell the deception. We'll wait and move in once the others show up."

"Marshal, you can't expect my men to stand guard out here without a fire of their own," Carson replied, his concern for his men evident.

"We'll rotate the watch," Hardin suggested. "Station two of your men close to the camp to keep an eye out until the rustlers show up and then signal the rest of us."

"Alright, that seems fair enough," Carson agreed. "Though I can't keep the men out here for long. Hardy and Reg, you two take the first watch. Set up the sleeping area to make it look like the rustler's bedded down for the night. And don't forget to bring his horse along—remove the saddle and position it on the other side of the blanket, and keep it visible."

"Got it, boss," Hardy replied. "How long do we keep watch?"

"Jess and Lane, you'll switch out in four hours," Carson added. "Does that work for you, Marshal?"

"Sounds fine," Hardin said.

As Hardy and Reg mounted their horses, Carson carried on. "Keep the fire burning and they'll think he's asleep. We'll be over the ridge at the camp, south of the canyon where we go during drives. We will wait there for news from one of you."

The two men nodded and rode away with the rustler's horse following behind them.

"Jess, take Lane and the marshal to that spot in the south canyon where we camp during our drives. Set us up where the rustlers can't see our fire. I'll grab some coffee and a pot and bring it there."

"Yes, sir," Jess replied, swinging onto his horse as the cowboys rode away, with Hardin following.

An hour later, near the old campsite they had used while working for Amos Cutler, Jess and Lane started a fire.

"I'm really glad the wind has calmed down tonight," Lane said, rubbing his hands near the flames.

"At least *we* have a fire to keep us warm," Jess replied. "Hardy and Reg have nothing but their coats."

Hardin crouched by the fire, listening to the two men and hoping this time they would finally catch the cattle rustlers who plagued the hardworking cowboys. With the new jail in Bitterroot Springs, Sheriff Shepard wouldn't have any excuses for botched escapes like before, as he wouldn't be in charge.

After a long while, a horse snorted from the edge of the woods, and Tom Carson rode into the clearing. "You men ready to brew some coffee?"

Jess hurried over to Carson and took the coffeepot from his hands. "I'll fetch us some water from the stream."

Carson secured his horse and sat down by the fire. "Marshal, we gotta wrap this up soon. We got cattle to move from the canyon."

Hardin looked at the foreman. "Winter's harsh on cattle."

"Yes, sir," Carson said. "We've already lost nine head to winter."

"How do you turn a profit when you're losing cattle like that?"

"Amos raises more than we need to make up for the loss. The only hitch in that plan is feeding them. So, the boss brought in two horse-drawn grass cutters last year. He hires temporary hands after the hay dries to rake it into bins."

"Yeah, they used those in Kansas," Hardin said. "Seems like a lot of work, but if you can store it properly, you'll have food for the herd through the winter."

Jess placed the coffeepot over the flames and settled down on the ground beside the others. Rubbing his hands together for warmth, he added, "We probably won't hear from those rustlers tonight."

"There's no way to be sure," Hardin replied. "They've kept a man at the camp for a reason. My guess is the others will show up—maybe they're planning another rustling job."

"I figure they'll hit tonight or tomorrow," Carson said. "Could you check that coffee, Jess?"

Jess wrapped a rag around the coffeepot's handle and poured a bit into a cup. "It looks good to me, Tom."

Hardin walked to his horse, grabbed his tin cup from the saddlebags, and returned to the fire.

Jess grinned when he saw it. "Now there's a man who enjoys his coffee. Do you always bring a cup along to camp, Marshal?

Hardin nodded with a grin. "Yeah, I'm *always* ready for coffee."

Carson looked up and saw one of his men moving into camp. "We may not have time to finish our coffee, fellows. Reg, what's going on?"

Reg approached the fire to warm himself. "Tom, two riders just rode in."

"Did they try to wake their man?" Carson asked.

"No, they still think he's asleep."

"Let's not take those two yet," Hardin said. "We'll get ourselves prepared for the others to show."

"Right," Carson replied, standing up and tossing the remains of his coffee into the flames. "Lead the way, Reg."

Reg stepped forward and guided them along a narrow trail to the edge of the woods, where Hardy waited in the shadows.

"They just added more wood to the fire," Hardy whispered. "They mentioned their friend sleeping, but didn't wake him."

"That's good," Hardin said, looking through the trees. "Let's spread out and watch for them. When I make my move, follow my lead."

Carson and his men quietly took their positions in the woods, surrounding the two rustlers as they waited for Hardin's signal.

Hardin fell back into the trees, keeping a keen watch on the scene. Thirty minutes later, three more riders rode in, dismounted beside the fire, and secured their horses.

Hardin waited to let them settle in. One man, clearly in charge, pulled out an envelope and began distributing money among the group. He then instructed one of them to wake the man sleeping. Hardin waited no longer and stepped out from the trees. "Get your hands up!" he demanded.

The rustlers froze at the sound of his voice, quickly complying, raising their hands when they spotted his gun. Carson and his men emerged from the woods with their guns drawn.

As Hardin moved closer to the rustlers, he recognized them in the low light. One was Matt Staap; the others were Dean Dunmore, and the brothers Boone and Wallace Rogers—those he had arrested before, who had escaped from Miles City's jail. To his utter surprise, the man giving out the money was Sheriff Bud Shepard.

"I can hardly believe my eyes," Hardin said, his voice laced with disbelief as he looked at the sheriff.

"What do you think you're onto, Marshal?" Shepard shot back defiantly. "Our business is *none* of your concern."

"On Cutler land?" Carson cut in sharply.

"This is still open range," Shepard argued.

"Every rancher knows where Amos' boundaries end," Carson responded. "The reason you're here is to pay off your rustlers."

"Prove it!" Shepard challenged, his glare fixed on Hardin.

"I believe I will," Hardin countered, moving toward the suspects' horses to search through their gear. He quickly found a branding iron tied to the back of Dean's horse, with the letters "MM." As he rummaged through the other saddlebags, he discovered over a hundred used cattle tags, evidence that left him shaking his head.

Returning to the campfire with the branding iron and saddlebags in hand, Hardin said, "Dean, you're going away for a long time."

"Marshal, do you think we have enough to keep them from getting off?" Carson inquired.

"I'll testify to the tracks I found," Hardin explained. "If the evidence we've got here matches up, then yes. Tie their hands and get them mounted on their horses."

"What about our other man?" Dean asked, sneering. If they were going to jail, he wanted to make sure Earl did too. "I can't believe that man's still sleeping."

Hardin marched over to the blanket and yanked the covers back, exposing the rocks they had used as a decoy. "You mean *this* man?" he asked, his voice mixed with sarcasm as he prodded at the stones with his boot.

"If Earl's not sleeping, where is he?" Dean asked.

"Earl's in jail at Bitterroot Springs, the same place *you're* headed," Hardin replied, noting the flicker of surprise that crossed Shepard's face. "That's right, Sheriff. There'll be no slipping out of this jail."

With the prisoners' hands securely tied, they put them on their horses and headed toward Bitterroot Springs.

29

The winter proved harsh, yet it had led to fewer bar brawls and cattle rustling incidents for Hardin to deal with. Snow still covered the ground, and today the sun shone brightly, giving the lawman an idea. He decided to ride over to Victoria's to check on her.

After saddling Amos, Hardin made his way through town, noticing that others shared the same impulse to venture out on the sunny day.

He soon arrived at Victoria's place and noticed smoke rising from the chimney. Beneath a shed, her new buggy sat, making him wonder why he hadn't seen her around town. In a nearby corral, her palomino mare galloped playfully when she spotted Amos.

He dismounted, tied Amos to a small tree, and walked to the front door. After knocking, he heard a sound from inside. Victoria soon opened the door, wrapped in a colorful quilt, her face marked by surprise at his presence.

"Victoria, how are you?" Hardin asked.

"Well, as you can tell, I'm just trying to stay warm," she replied. "Please come in."

She led him toward the kitchen. "I knew winters could be terrible in Montana, but I never expected this year to be one of the worst. I'm so glad to see the sun out today. Would you like some coffee?"

"Sure. Though I can't stay long," Hardin replied.

Victoria set a coffeepot on the kitchen stove. "I have plenty of room for your horse—there are three stalls in my small barn. I wasn't sure if I might want another horse, so I had the carpenters build it a bit larger than necessary. And Reuben, I have an extra room in the house if you'd like to stay here... through the winter, I mean."

"I'll think about it. Why don't you sit?" Hardin suggested.

Her eyes sparkled as she walked closer. "Have you missed me?"

"I have," he replied. "The winter is gloomy and hard on the horses."

"The horses?" she asked, curiously.

"Err, when I saw the sun shining this morning," he added, a smile forming, "I thought of you and figured I should come see you."

"So, Reuben, is this part of your duties to check on all the women in the territory? Or maybe you suspect that I robbed one of the banks in town?" Victoria teased.

"Or the freight office," Hardin countered with a playful grin.

Victoria leaned in and kissed him for a long while. "You can check on me anytime," she said, as she rose to add a few sticks of wood to the kitchen stove. "I can't believe how quickly wood burns in these things."

"You have a spacious house. Trying to heat it all can be quite a challenge," Hardin noted.

She poured him a cup of coffee, then filled her own. "I wasn't joking about you staying here, Reuben."

"I know you weren't, and I'm seriously considering your offer," Hardin replied. "My only concern is for myself. I try to live by the Good

Book, which means I believe in abstaining from inappropriate relations with a woman until after marriage. Staying here might test that commitment."

"I understand that better than you might think, Reuben. My uncle is a minister, and we attended his church in St. Louis when I was young."

"Is that where you're from?" he asked, intrigued.

Victoria took a sip of her coffee and responded, "Father served as a physician for the Union during the war. I don't remember much from that time, but I do recall how deeply it affected him. After the war ended, he relocated us from Hickory, North Carolina, to take a position as a surgeon at a hospital in St. Louis, though he was never quite the same afterward. His condition slowly deteriorated, and he began experiencing delusions. Eventually, my mother had him admitted to an asylum, and he passed away a year later."

"I'm sorry to hear that. Where is your mother now?" Hardin asked.

Victoria leaned on her elbow against the table. "From what I last heard, she's living in North Carolina with her sister. Perhaps I'll get to see her again before she leaves this world."

"I'm sure you will," he replied, glancing down at the wood chips scattered beside the stove. "Where do you keep your firewood? I'll bring some in for you."

"Thank you," Victoria said. "It's under the shed by the buggy—at least the wood that's already split. I still have quite a bit of work there to do."

Hardin got up from his chair and put on his coat. "I'll be back in with an armload," he said.

Victoria watched as he made his way to the shed, where he noticed that only a few sticks of split wood were available. After brushing off the snow, he located the axe and started to work. In about thirty minutes, he had stacked a sizable pile under the shed and carried a couple of armloads inside, setting them down with a satisfied sigh.

"I didn't mean for you to do *my* work," Victoria said.

"You should have asked for my help," Hardin replied with a smile. "I would have been happy to split it *all* for you."

She reached up, her touch light as she pressed a kiss to his cheek. "You're truly a good man, you know."

He shook his head. "Not really. There's too much grim history in my past."

"You just told me how you try to live by the Good Book. Doesn't it say to live by faith? Trusting God is not only for the future, but to help us overcome the past too."

Hardin was shocked to hear her say those words. She mentioned that she had gone to church as a child, but he hadn't realized she was a Christian. "You're right," he admitted. "We walk by faith, not by sight. Yet, it's human nature for us to hold on to things of the past."

He had confessed to the life he'd taken in Hays City, but it seemed Victoria sought to influence his heart in another direction. Her father had taught her that dwelling too much on the past could lead a person to a dark place. Ironically, that was a lesson he himself had never fully heeded.

"Why don't we do something outside?" Victoria suggested with a smile.

"In the snow?" Hardin responded. "I thought you were cold."

"Reuben, I have *you* to keep me warm. So, let's get away—in the buggy. Why don't you get my horse and hitch him up while I get ready, and we'll head to town?"

He gazed at her questioningly. "To town?"

"Yes," Victoria confirmed. "I could use some supplies, and you could pick up your clothes from the hotel and stay here with me for a few days."

Hardin gave only a moment of thought. "Alright, let's do it," he agreed.

Once Hardin had the horse and buggy ready, they set off for town. Their first stop was the café, where they enjoyed lunch together. Afterward, Hardin went to collect his clothes from the hotel, while Victoria handed a list of supplies to Charles Stewart, the owner of the general store, so he could gather everything she needed. As he waited, Hardin took a moment to send a telegram to William Boyd, inquiring about when he could leave Montana. Once

Charles had loaded Victoria's items into the buggy, they made their way back to her place.

Hardin remained with Victoria for over a week as winter storms continued to sweep through Montana. As the weather began to improve, Hardin remarked it was time for him to get to work. Victoria cooked a special meal for him, hoping the gesture would express her warmth and make him feel welcome in her home.

As they sat down at the table for the meal, Victoria glanced across at Hardin. "There's something I need to tell you before you leave," she said.

Hardin felt that he knew her well enough that nothing would truly surprise him, but this news caught him off guard.

"I might be leaving Bitterroot Springs," she confessed.

"Leaving? Where are you going?" he asked, stunned.

With frustration on her face, she said, "Reuben, I'm struggling to establish myself as a doctor here. I've been in this town for nearly nine months, but I rarely treat more than one patient a week. My funds are dwindling rapidly at the bank. If I don't do something soon, I'll be broke."

He looked into her eyes and replied, "I can help spread the word. There's a newspaper—perhaps you could run some ads, or we could ask Sara Harlan to write a story about the good work you've done."

She shook her head, glancing away briefly. When she turned back to him, she said, "I invested most of my savings into this place, but now I need to sell it. It would make a perfect small ranch for a family."

Hardin felt a deep ache inside. Victoria was the first woman he had ever felt truly at ease with. She comprehended his work because her profession shared similar qualities in helping others. He had to consider whether leaving Montana might give them a chance to be together.

With a wistful look in his eyes, he studied her face and murmured, "I have something else to confess. I came to Montana to prove my skills as a lawman, hoping that my efforts would eventually lead to a chance to become a sheriff again in a small town."

"So you're saying if they are satisfied with your work, you might leave Montana, too?" Victoria replied. "That means we could be together."

Hardin shrugged his shoulders. "Only that *my* leaving isn't definite."

"Neither is mine," Victoria replied, "though I've submitted applications for doctor positions in several small towns in Kansas and Nebraska. Then I received an invitation to apply for a position in Dodge City, Kansas, where they badly need a doctor. I've submitted my application to their city council, but I haven't received a response from them."

"Well, the stage hasn't run in about a month," Hardin responded. "When it does, I'm sure you'll hear something."

"Yes," she said.

"So, you might have the chance to work in Dodge?" Hardin asked.

Victoria stood up from her chair and walked over to him. Hardin pushed back his chair to make room, and she settled herself in his lap.

"I would never leave if I could make it work here," Victoria said. "The winters are terrible, but I truly cherish your being here with me. You've been an unexpected breath of fresh air in my life, and I'm grateful for that."

"I enjoy being with you, too," Hardin replied. "I hoped... that one day we might marry."

"I would love to marry you, as long as we can spend time together," she expressed. "But I won't stand in the way of you finding someone who will treat you well. If I leave Montana and you're still here, will you please keep your heart open to others?"

"I'm not sure I can," Hardin replied, forcing a smile. "You're the only woman who truly understands me."

"Reuben, don't be so quick to dismiss other women," she urged gently. "Keep your heart open, and God will fill it."

Her words resonated like a prophecy in Hardin's ears. Among all the women in Bitter-root Springs and Miles City, Victoria was the only one who ever captured his heart.

He gently eased her from his lap and stood. "I think I should gather my things and head back to town."

"You don't have to leave just because you're going back to work," Victoria said.

"I know, but I've got an office at the jail now," Hardin replied. "The mayor would prefer I be there when I can, and he could give a bad report to William Boyd. If I find myself riding east for work, I might stop and visit."

She nodded with a huge smile. "I would love that."

He quickly gathered his belongings and tossed them into his saddlebags. After sharing one last passionate kiss, he headed to the barn to saddle Amos.

Victoria stood on the back steps, watching him wave as he rode away, her heart filled with a mix of hope and sadness.

30

The carpenters worked diligently to install the new sign at the jail while many towns-folk gathered to watch. Hardin stood alongside Mayor Glenn Barlow, watching as they hammered the final nail.

"Well, Mayor, you did it," Hardin remarked.

"It's hard to believe it's finally finished, but here it stands," Barlow replied. "We overcame opposition from two council members and struggled to find a qualified sheriff, but we've succeeded."

"It's a fine jail too," Hardin agreed.

As the carpenters stepped back and put away their tools, the crowd burst into applause, marking the milestone.

Barlow turned and called forward a new-comer to Bitterroot Springs. "Attention, everyone! I want to introduce our new sheriff, Mr.

Virgil Hancock. Let's give him a warm welcome to Bitterroot Springs, Montana."

The crowd responded with enthusiastic applause for Sheriff Hancock, a man in his mid-fifties. He wore two guns at his hips, light-colored britches, and a brown vest over a solid green shirt. His neatly trimmed, partially gray hair and mustache gave him a seasoned appearance. On his head rested a well-worn brown Stetson hat.

Sheriff Hancock waved and smiled at the crowd. "Thank you all for your warm welcome. I assure you I'll do everything in my power to reduce crime here. But, I must inform you that a new ordinance in the coming days will limit guns to law enforcement within city limits."

A wave of boos rippled through the crowd, primarily from the men.

"Now, hold on," Hancock said, raising a hand to calm the crowd. "This doesn't mean you can't own a gun. Just please leave it at home when you come to town. If you forget and arrive wearing one, you can leave it at the jail until you're ready to leave."

A man in the midst of the crowd raised his hand. "What if you live in town?"

"I'm sorry, sir, but no one should carry a gun in town unless you work for the law," Hancock replied firmly.

More boos erupted from the crowd.

Hardin stepped forward, raising a hand to silence them. "Hold on a minute, folks. Let me speak." The crowd gradually quieted. "I get your concerns, but remember, you elected these council members to ensure your safety. Storing your guns at the jail while handling business or enjoying a drink is a small price to pay for maintaining peace, wouldn't you agree?"

The crowd murmured, echoing a collective "yes."

"So you understand," Hardin continued. "Then help your sheriff do his job to keep the peace."

A voice called from the back, "What about me, Marshal Hardin? You gonna try to take my gun?"

Hardin locked eyes with a young man on horseback at the edge of the crowd. He wore an oddly shaped dark hat and a brown leather vest. As the crowd parted, his holstered revolver on his hip came into view.

The cowboy dismounted, tied his horse to the hitching rail, and turned to face Hardin with a determined glare. "You were the lawman on duty when my brother was gunned down in the saloon," he said firmly.

"You'd be Jedediah McCray," Hardin replied.

The cowboy smiled and said, "So, you remembered my name. I thought you might play ignorant."

"Dying isn't something easily forgotten," Hardin said, keeping a watchful eye on him in case he drew his gun.

"That's right, and I won't forget that you were in charge that night, Marshal," Jedediah said, his tone unwavering.

"Jedediah, I didn't kill your brother," Hardin remarked, trying to defuse the tension.

"No, but you didn't stop it either!" Jedediah shouted, his voice rising. "When you leave your kinfolk behind to go chase after cattle, you expect the law will protect them. You didn't, Marshal—you let him die."

"This town is not my responsibility, though I help when I can," Hardin countered. "Searching the trails for criminals is more what I do."

"I don't care!" Jedediah replied. walking to the center of the street. "You'd better get ready, because I came here to kill you, Marshal."

"Don't you think a gunfight is taking revenge too far? I arrested the man responsible for your brother's death," Hardin said, hoping to appeal to reason.

Jedediah sneered, "But you let him go free—the man who took my brother's life."

Hardin responded, "Your brother drew on him first. That man had no choice."

"Marshal, do you think that makes a difference to me? Jedediah shouted, his anger growing.

"I don't want to fight you, Jedediah. No one needs to get hurt today," Hardin said earnestly.

The cowboy fell silent, his eyes fixed on Hardin, his hand poised over his weapon.

Although Hardin was skilled with a gun, he had limited experience in gunfights, having faced only a few men in his life and evading them whenever possible. But the glint in Jedediah's eyes signaled an inevitable showdown. "Don't do this, son," Hardin pleaded one last time.

The cowboy licked his lips and suddenly drew his weapon from the holster. But before Jedediah could fire, Hardin pulled the trigger on his gun, striking the cowboy's shoulder that held the firearm.

Jedediah let go of his weapon and fell to his knees, staring up at Hardin. "Better kill me now, Marshal. I'll come back for you."

"Don't follow your brother's path—you don't have to die," Hardin replied. He turned to the crowd and shouted, "Someone get Dr. Hawkins!"

As Mayor Barlow scanned for a rider to fetch the doctor, a young woman from the saloon hurried out with a rag to staunch Jedediah's bleeding.

Sheriff Hancock approached Hardin. "Marshal, don't let this bother you—you gave him every chance to walk away."

"His brother was in the wrong and paid the price," Hardin said. "Maybe someday Jedediah will understand."

"I doubt it—it's tough to know what drives some men," Hancock replied.

Barlow noticed their exchange and approached. "Gentlemen, surely I didn't expect a gunfight. At least you stopped it, though we can't let this spoil our celebration."

"Yeah, it's over for now," Hardin said, looking down at the young cowboy.

"Well, we're still having the dance," Barlow added. "I won't let this derail our plans."

"Sure, everything's under control now," Sheriff Hancock replied. "I'll lock the young man up once the doctor's done with his wound."

Hardin glanced up just in time to see a cowboy riding toward them with Dr. Hawkins on a horse beside him. They dismounted, handed their horses' reins to someone nearby, and the doctor quickly assessed the injured man, instructing the crowd to move him to a dry area.

"There are beds in the jail," Sheriff Hancock suggested. "Might as well take him there—it's where he'll end up once he's healed."

As they carried the injured man to the jail, Hardin walked up alongside Victoria. "They're holding a dance tonight to celebrate the new jail. Would you care to join me?"

Victoria shot a brief smile as she continued walking, "Sure, if you'll hitch my buggy."

He nodded with a grin. "I think I can handle that. Be there before dark," he replied, watching as the doctor went into the jail to attend to the patient.

With the dance starting in only a few hours, Hardin decided he should freshen up. He headed to the hotel, where he requested a bath, and then headed upstairs to wait.

31

The mayor's invitation to the dance proved a resounding success. People from all parts of Bitterroot Springs came for the celebration. Buggies and wagons crowded the area around the livery, with horses tethered to hitch rails at that end of town.

Volunteers had transformed the livery's hallway into a dance space. Around the open area, tables featured an array of cakes, pies, and punch, served by the ladies' group from the church. Local musicians had come to provide music for the evening.

Hardin found a suitable spot to park the buggy, then he and Victoria made their way to the door. "Looks like the whole town has shown up," he noted.

"I'm sure there'll be plenty I've never met," Victoria replied.

As the band struck up an upbeat melody, they headed inside with others flocking to the dance floor.

"Over there are some hay bales we can sit on," Hardin suggested.

"Sure," Victoria replied. "I wish now I hadn't picked this dress."

"You look fantastic," he assured her, holding her hand as she sat. "Would you like some punch?"

"That would be great," she responded.

He headed over to the second table, where a sweet elderly woman dipped out punch for two.

"You made it," a voice said from behind him.

Hardin turned and saw Sheriff Hancock in line behind him. "Oh, yes. It's a great chance to meet folks I've never seen before."

"I figure the mayor cooked this up after hiring me," Hancock replied. "But I heard you're still pretty new around here."

"About nine months," Hardin said.

"Nine months?" Hancock repeated, edging forward in line. "You ought to know most people by now."

Hardin turned back to look at him. "I don't work in Bitterroot Springs all the time."

"I suppose that's true," Hancock replied with a nod, "seeing as you're a territorial Marshal and all."

"That's right," Hardin added. "Excuse me, I've got someone waiting for these refreshments."

Sheriff Hancock glanced down the row of bales and spotted Victoria sitting alone. "I reckon you don't want to waste time jawing with an old coot like me, do ya?" He chuckled heartily as Hardin walked off with the punch.

Hardin reached Victoria and handed her the refreshment. "Couldn't get away from the new sheriff."

"Oh, that was him?" she asked.

"Yes, Sheriff Hancock," Hardin replied. "How about we share a dance once we've finished our punch?"

"I'd love to."

They watched as the young men asked the ladies to dance, and how the parents intervened if they disapproved. After a few tunes, the band played a slow melody. Hardin offered his hand, and Victoria gladly joined him in the dance area.

Smiling at her, he said, "I've been thinking about this all day."

"But I may be leaving soon, so let's not let things get out of hand," she replied.

He gazed into her eyes. "It's just a dance, my dear."

She laughed. "I suppose I was presuming. I do have a question, though."

"Of course."

Victoria frowned, scanning the crowd. "How do people in Bitterroot get medical attention when they're sick or injured? I've been here five months, and I feel like I've only scratched the surface."

"There's no doctor in Bitterroot besides you," Hardin replied. "But I've heard Faye Rogers—the one who runs the boarding house helps—folks who are sick. She used to work as a nurse for a doctor back in Denver."

"Hmm, that's news to me. Why is this the first I'm hearing about it?"

"You got me," Hardin replied, gazing into her eyes. "You mentioned that you might be leaving. So, have you heard anything more?"

Victoria paused mid-dance. "Let me grab my shawl, and we'll step outside to talk.

As she turned toward the hay, Hardin stood, watching her and wondering if he had said something wrong. She reached for the shawl, and then they stepped outside.

"It's already cooling down," Victoria said as a shiver ran through her. "Shall we head to the buggy? It might block some of the breeze."

"Sure," he replied.

They settled into the buggy, and Victoria pulled out the blanket she'd brought for the ride home. "That's much better."

"You never answered my question." Hardin pressed gently.

Victoria met his gaze, a knot of dread tightening in her stomach. "Okay, the letter from the Dodge City Council arrived last week. I've been hired and can start as soon as I arrive."

"Congratulations, Victoria," Hardin said, shifting slightly away from her. "That's what you wanted, right?"

"Well, I would've preferred St. Louis or Kansas City, but yes, it sounds like a great opportunity."

"Certainly," he murmured, his eyes fixed on the buggy floor.

"Reuben, I'm sorry to be leaving so soon after we met," Victoria said, noticing the sadness etched on his face. "I'm nearly broke and don't really have a choice. I'll struggle with a lack of funds, so there's little I can do except try to sell."

"It'll sell eventually," he answered quietly. "Um, why don't I take you home before it gets too cold?"

They had only been at the dance for an hour, but Victoria could see Hardin had lost all interest in the dance after her announcement. "Yeah, that's fine. It is turning cool."

The fifteen-minute ride back to her place felt like two hours as they sat in the buggy in silence. Victoria feared saying anything that might deepen the wound in his heart, while Hardin silently berated himself for the foolish mistake that had tied him to Montana—the day he killed the Gitton boy.

When they reached Victoria's house, Hardin dropped her off and quickly unhitched the buggy. In a matter of minutes, he saddled Amos and rode away without another word.

As he entered the town and spotted the weathered name sign, nagging questions came to mind: Why was the town called Bitterroot Springs? Was it due to the residents' bitter experiences from barely surviving, or perhaps some mystical element had been sprinkled in the water? The place seemed to Hardin nothing more than a frigid, dark, and lonely stretch of land better off left to the Indians.

Hardin led Amos to the back of the livery stable while the music and the dance continued inside. He unsaddled the horse and released him into the corral with the others, knowing that Ezra would tend to him in the morning.

After leaving the livery, Hardin headed to the hotel and quickly climbed the stairs. In his room, he shrugged off his coat and hurled it across the room, knocking the picture of President Lincoln from the wall. Spotting his gun and holster hanging at the headboard, he snatched it and flung it away in frustration.

Staring at the weapon on the floor, he muttered, "If it weren't for you, I wouldn't be in this mess."

He sank onto the bed, kicked off his boots, and sent them crashing against the door. Burying his face in his hands, he craved some whiskey, convinced a single drink could dull the raw pain throbbing inside him.

At last, he lay back on the bed, his thoughts pressing down like a weight on his chest as he stared at the ceiling. He wished, if only for a moment, that the Montana Territory—and the bittersweet ache in his heart—could vanish just for a little while.

Hours passed in restless meditation. As shadows in the room deepened, Hardin's eyelids grew heavy, and he finally drifted off to sleep.

32

Morning arrived, and Hardin lingered in bed until he could stand it no longer. With a sigh, he threw back the covers and perched on the edge, staring out the window as the town below awakened. He spotted the morning stage sitting at the home office, which signaled it was nearly eleven o'clock.

He pulled on his britches and stood by the window, watching Lydia Travers and her companion beside the stage, as if poised to board. Perhaps her man told her what she wanted to hear, he mused.

Glancing at the telegraph office, Hardin recalled he hadn't yet heard from William Boyd. Resolving to send another message, he quickly finished dressing, splashed water on his face, strapped on his gun, and stepped out of the room.

As Hardin strode into the street, Caleb Holt and Tom Carson rode by, tipping their hats in a friendly wave. Heading the opposite direction, undertaker Eli Whitaker rumbled past in his wagon, a casket secured in the back.

He entered the telegraph office, where Abe Tucker was busy jotting down an incoming message as the machine clattered away. Once finished, Abe looked up. "Hello, Marshal."

"Abe, I've got another message to send," Hardin said.

"Got another prisoner to go after, Marshal?" Abe asked, slipping the paper into an envelope.

"Not today."

Abe turned and looked up at him. "So what do you... Oh, wait a minute." He rose from his chair, walked to a cabinet, and pulled out a piece of paper. "I should have gotten this to you yesterday. Sorry, I had forgotten about it. We were so busy, and I never saw you." He handed it to Hardin.

The marshal looked over the paper, which read:

I know we talked about your coming home after some time in Montana, but I can't let you go to Kansas right now. My boss is insisting that I keep you there for a while. We'll revisit the situation in about a year from now. And please, refrain from sending telegrams—they'll only make you seem desperate. Sincerely, William Boyd, Director of the U.S. Marshal Services.

Hardin turned toward the door.

"Don't you want to send a telegram, Marshal?" Abe Tucker asked.

"No need now," Hardin replied. "Got my answer."

Hardin's anger surged as he strode toward the hotel. He was at a crossroads, with two stark choices: quit his marshal post and ride south to seek new opportunities, or endure the frigid Montana winters until Boyd finally allowed him to return home.

He walked down the street until he could step onto the boardwalk as the town around him bustled with people stocking up on supplies. Grover French was unloading a couple of wagons of freight at the general store and waved as the marshal passed, but Hardin scarcely acknowledged him.

Reaching the restaurant, he found it was less crowded than expected, so he ordered the special and ate quickly, eager to avoid lingering. With his decision weighing on him, he returned to his room, packed his belongings into a small bag, grabbed his rifle, and checked out.

He ducked into the general store for essentials, then headed to the livery stable. After settling his debt with Ezra, he saddled Amos and rode eastward, with no specific destination in mind.

Riding past the sawmill, Hardin mulled over job prospects in Kansas. Could he end up as a timberman? Or perhaps find a position laying tracks for the railroad? Cattle drives were dwindling, and with the railroad's arrival, ranchers had likely filled any cowhand openings. One thing was clear: abandoning the marshal service might wipe out his law-man career forever.

He reached a familiar spot along the Powder River, where he had once camped. With hours of daylight remaining, he debated stopping or riding on, anxious that passersby might intrude on his thoughts.

As Hardin gazed away from the river, he spotted an old trail snaking through the landscape. He urged Amos forward and noticed a few unshod tracks—likely from Indian ponies—winding into the trees. The path was narrow but navigable.

After about thirty minutes, he emerged into an opening and heard the rush of water, possibly the river or a creek branching from it. He dismounted to survey the area. "Amos, this seems like a good spot to camp, as long as no Indians pass through."

He unsaddled Amos and tied him with a long rope for grazing, then gathered dry branches and stacked them near the old fire pit. Venturing into the woods, he located a small creek a few hundred feet away, where three mallards burst into flight at the sound of his footsteps in the leaves. He returned to camp, led Amos to the creek, and secured him nearby. "There you go, buddy—have some water."

In a short while, he had the campfire lit and set the coffee pot on to heat it. He settled on a fallen old oak tree, then reached into his saddlebags, pulling out his Bible. As the coffee finished making, he poured a cup and opened the Good Book to a passage in Proverbs. He read it aloud: *"Trust in the Lord with all thine heart; and lean not unto thine own understanding. In all thy ways acknowledge him, and he shall direct thy paths."*

Closing his eyes, Hardin bowed his head in prayer. "Lord, there's no denying my understanding falls short. I thought a fresh start in Montana would be good for me—I met a wonderful woman here and fell in love. But her leaving has turned everything upside down. Now, like when I killed the Gittens boy, all I see is darkness. This has dragged me to a low place again. I don't know where this path leads and if I quit and head to Kansas, I may never be a lawman again. Surely, Montana isn't my final destiny."

Hardin paused, listening intently for any sign of an answer from above. After a few moments, he continued his prayer: "Lord, I just read your word—it says to trust you with all my heart and not lean on my own understanding. You know I've always wanted to be a lawman, just a sheriff in a quiet town. I don't enjoy in chasing bandits through this wilderness, but if this is your path, I'll follow it. Help me trust your ways so I can move beyond my doubts."

He took a couple of sips of coffee as he re-examined the passage once more. "Lord, take my mind in your hands and guide my path."

Amos nickered softly, drawing Hardin's attention, to the faint footsteps in the woods. Possibly Indians, he thought. With tension rising inside him, he grabbed his rifle and chambered a round.

A voice echoed from the trees: "Hello, in the camp. Can I come in?"

"Show yourself," Hardin replied.

A moment later, Silas Granger stepped out from the trees, his familiar figure cutting through the shadows. "Oh, it's you, pilgrim," Silas said with a nod.

"Come on in," Hardin replied, though he really wanted privacy.

Silas glanced at the glowing campfire. "I seem to be drawn to your camp, Marshal. The air around you always has that hint of coffee," he said, eyeing the pot.

"Help yourself."

Silas pulled a cup from his pack, watching Hardin carefully. "Hmm, pilgrim, you look in a sad way today."

Hardin didn't reply, careful not to share his trouble.

Silas poured himself a cup of coffee, then raised back up, his gaze steady on his marshal friend. "Marshal, I learned long ago that light can be painful to find. If a man dwells in darkness more than he does the light, he won't easily recognize light when it comes around."

Hardin lifted his head and met the old trapper's gaze, noting how his words echoed something near to scripture. "I believe I've read something like that in the Bible."

Silas took a sip of coffee and chuckled. "Ah, you city folks aren't the only ones who read the Good Book. Now, how about sharing your troubles with a friend?"

Hardin shook his head briefly, but recounted the events, the message from William Boyd, and his shattered hopes. "I thought that when I left Montana," he continued, "it would be for my next sheriff's job in a small Kansas town."

"When you learned you couldn't go, I reckon it hit you hard," Silas said warmly.

"Yes, but...I met a woman in Bitterroot, a doctor I really like," Hardin said. "I thought we were growing closer, but she told me she's leaving for a job in Dodge City—she might be gone by now."

"I can't help you there; I've had no luck with women myself," Silas replied. "But if you love being a lawman so much, nothing should stand in your way. If you think leaving will hurt your chances at that path, why go?"

Silas's words resonated deeply, aligning with the passage of scripture from Proverbs he had just read. Had the Lord sent this old man by to speak wisdom because he wasn't hearing him?

"Thank you, Silas," Hardin replied. "What you said is true. I'm sure my anger's clouding my judgment."

"You know, I'm not a smart man," Silas added, "my daddy always said I wasn't. But what if you left Montana and the right woman—the one God Almighty meant for you—shows up here?"

Lean not on your own understanding, Hardin thought. God knew exactly what he needed to hear. "You know, Silas," he said, a smile forming, "I believe I'm staying in Montana. I'll ride back to Bitterroot Springs tonight. Maybe I can get my room back at the hotel."

"Then don't let me hold you up, Pilgrim," Silas replied. "I need to mosey down the river anyway, and put out a few more traps before dark." He stood, tossed the cold coffee from his cup, and stowed it in his pack. "I'll see you around, Marshal."

"Yes, it seems you will," Hardin said with a smile.

As Hardin watched Silas disappear into the trees, he packed his belongings and saddled Amos. Mounting quickly, he turned toward the river. Darkness would fall by the time he arrived, but it didn't matter—he knew his path, at least for now. Had he trusted God sooner, he might not have seen Montana as so miserable and remote.

Thank you so much for reading **Montana Lawman!** I truly hope you enjoyed the story. If you did, I would greatly appreciate it if you could take a moment to leave a review on Amazon. Your honest feedback not only helps other readers find the book but also guides them in deciding if it's a good fit for them. Your opinion means so much to me, and it only takes a moment of your time. Michael Spanhanks

To leave your review, scan the QR code.

About The Author

Author Michael Spanhanks writes exciting stories across various genres, including action-packed adventures, historical westerns, post-apocalyptic tales, and thrilling suspense novels. Now retired after 27 years in the tire industry, he enjoys quiet mornings creating captivating fiction while sipping on his favorite cup of coffee.

Look for these book and series on Amazon
Journey From The Wilderness—3 Books series
Stalls Family Historical Westerns—3 Book series
Laura Stone Mysteries—standalone short stories
Mystery of the Lakes—3 Book series
Marshal Reuben Hardin Historical Westerns—3 Book series

Michael's Books

PRODIGAL TRAIL - Book 1 in the Stalls Family Historical Westerns Series

Leaving home was the plan. Killing a man in a gunfight never played into it.

Jesse Stalls and his friend Billy Cantrell purchased Colt .45s, preparing to leave home on a cattle drive. Not freezing rain, thieves, or mountain lions could make them return to farming. However, plans never turn out as expected.

The cattle drive ends at Fort Worth. Standing up for another cowhand, Jesse gets into a shoot-out with a man named Max Toliver. When the smoke clears, Toliver lies dead. His passing sends Jesse into a downward spiral and sets him up as the latest fast gun in the territory.

Jesse's no gunfighter, only a fortuitous young man who put his life on the line for a friend. Still, the news of Toliver's death spreads quickly and the name of the man guilty of it.

Jesse rides away, uncertain about his future. His venture brings him face to face with Mexican bandits who've kidnapped three women. During the skirmish, he befriends beautiful Hanna Elrod. As their friendship grows, Hanna realizes Jesse still anguishes over a gunfight. Jesse's faith plummets further, but she refuses to give up on him.

Can Jesse ever find God's love and forgiveness? Can the woman he's falling in love with point him back to God?

SAMUEL SON OF JESSE - Book 2 in the Stalls Family Historical Westerns Series
Samuel is furious over a horse deal his father Jesse makes. He leaves the Stalls' ranch in Booneville, Arkansas, with three friends for work in Kansas.

When they arrive at JA McFadden's Ranch, the ranch owner hires them as bronc busters, but the landowner's primary reason for hiring them is their proficiency with weapons—particularly Samuel. However, when McFadden asks the young cowboy to eliminate a neighboring rancher's foreman, it sends an obvious message that it's time for Samuel to move on.

Samuel is unfamiliar with the people nearby and camps in the vicinity without realizing he's on the Riverview land. The property owner's daughter, Maggie Rivers, notices him the next day, searching for food. Presuming he is an employee of McFadden, she shoots him in the shoulder. Compassion surfaces when she sees the young cowboy's injury. She gets him to the ranch, removes the bullet, and patches him up.

But when a brewing conflict between ranches seems imminent, what choice will Samuel make? Use his gun in defense of the ranch he now works for or pursue another path God has for him.

REBECCA DAUGHTER OF JESSE - Book 3 in the Stalls Family Historical Westerns Series

A once-in-a-lifetime adventure takes a deadly turn. A stubborn writer on an arduous wagon journey. Deeper into a wilderness of unexpected twists.

To understand the struggles women face on the Oregon Trail, Rebecca Stalls is determined to undertake a formidable wagon train journey West. Her dream is to write a book that details every conflict and heartbreak they have encountered. Not even threats of flooding rivers, bears, thieves, or the risk of human abduction can make her turn back—until she's finally faced enough.

From the moment they turn the wagon around, they are battered by cold and snow. The initial challenges are trivial in comparison to the trouble that follows.

Can Rebecca find the strength to endure the difficulties until she reaches safety? Will her faith remain in her moment of desperation?

Embark on an incredible journey today with Rebecca, Daughter of Jesse, book 3 and the final installment of the Stalls Family Historical Westerns saga.

THE CURIOSITY OF LAURA STONE

Laura Stone spent the past six years away from her family farm, focusing on advancing her education and building a career in journalism. Her return to Santa Fe was intended to be brief, but something about her father Horace Stone's passing seems suspicious. After hearing the sheriff's peculiar account, her journalistic instincts compel her to investigate what the law failed to do.

Her greatest surprise coming home is meeting a man who greatly appeases her emotions. But one major obstacle to a potentially wonderful relationship is his traditional views on marriage.

Will Laura uncover the truth about her father's death? What reason led men to his

land in the first place? Is romance brewing for the inquisitive journalist from Boston?

Dive into these six captivating, action-packed, and dramatic short stories, brimming with mystery, love, adventure, unexpected twists, and challenges as Laura Stone seeks to uncover the facts.

ASSASSIN'S ARROW - Book I in the Journey from The Wilderness Series

A young man of faith at a crossroads. When faced with an unexpected adversary, can he mend fences to heal America's shattered soul?

Travis Weston struggles to provide for his small community. Raised in the relative safety of the southern U.S. after executive orders urged Christians to flee the north or face death or imprisonment, the now twenty-year-old grew up dedicated to providing for family and friends. But when he stumbles across a hooded rival who stole his deer, he's shocked to discover the archer behind the bow is a beautiful woman.

Taking a chance by striking up a conversation, the suspicious hunter warms to her offer of laying down their weapons and sharing the kill. With the surprise igniting his belief that restoring liberty hinges on the creation of a united force, he prays he can serve as an inspiration to overcome the army of the North.

Can Travis forge a peace built on forgiveness and God's word?

The Assassin's Arrow is the thought-provoking first book in the Journey From The Wilderness post-apocalyptic thriller series. If you like action-packed everyman heroes, powerful Christian themes, and reaching for hope, then you'll love this profound tale.

BOOK 2 of the series is scheduled for release in 2026.

BOOK 3 of the series is scheduled for release in 2027.

Character list

Male characters
Reuben Hardin – main character and territorial marshal
Bud Shepard – sheriff at Miles City
Wade Norman – a deputy at Miles City
Ike McInnes – a rancher at Miles City
Nathaniel Boone – a rancher at Miles City
Shelton Quinn – the judge at Miles City
Glenn Barlow – mayor at Bitterroot Springs
Grant Walls – Vance's foreman
Cornelius Vance – a rancher who swindles timber cutters
William Boyd – Director of the U.S. Marshal Services
Jonathan Starks – dating Sarah Harlan, works at the bank
Charles Stewart – owner of general store at Bitterroot Springs

Grover French – freight man and wagon master

Josiah Reed – #1 leads timbermen outside Bitterroot Springs

Duncan Malloy – #2 timberman

Caleb Warrick – #3 timberman

Tim Forde – works for Amos Cutler/kills a man at a gunfight

Obie Judd – works for Amos Cutler/took bullet at a gunfight

Amos Cutler – rancher started new bank at Bitterroot Springs

Zeke Kane – Killed a man at a saloon/works for Culter Ranch

Gideon Walsh – elderly cowhand who works for Cutler Ranch

Caleb Holt – works for Cutler/brings word of a gunfight

Tom Carson – witnessed a shooting/foreman for Amos Cutler

Gideon Holt – owns the Bitterroot Trust Bank

Ezra Tate – livery man at Bitterroot

Harold Wightman – owns the mercantile at Miles City

Ted Bond – outlaw escapee

Hawk Blackthorn – half–Apache tracker riding with Ted Bond

Dean Dunmore – rustler #1

Boone Rogers – rustler #2

Wallace Rogers – rustler #3

Matt Staap – rustler #4

Earl Croy – rustler #5

Gus Simmons – Vance's gunman #1

Wesley Durant – Vance's gunman #2

Abner Cole – older cowhand at Vance's ranch

Elijah Stone – Vance's man/warns Hardin of fight

Rufus Hale – stockyard tender at Miles City

Tobias Finch – liveryman at Miles City

Colonel Miles – over Fort Miles

Nayati – leader of the small Nez Perce tribe

Kyle Gittens – young boy who died at Hays City

Wayne Gittens – the boy's father and mayor of Hays City

Thaddeus Morrow – Hardin's deputy at Hays City

James Moore – a rancher from Miles City/friend of Reuben

Colt Jackson – Moore's foreman/helps Hardin find escapees

Choro – James Moore's cowhand and tracker

Horace Aiken – owner of Traders Place

Jedediah McCray – brother of Levi McCray, and gunman

Virgil Hancock – new sheriff at Bitterroot Springs

Wylie Barton – witnessed rustled cattle at his ranch

Levi McCray – died when Zeke Kane shot him at the saloon

Tobias Redd – young cowboy/gunman at saloon

Eli Whitaker – undertaker at Bitterroot Springs

Solomon Burke – doctor at Miles City

Hiram Steele – a cowboy breaking a horse at Cutler's ranch

Rufus Clay – a cowboy helping Hiram to break the horse

Abe Tucker – telegraph operator at Bitterroot Springs

Jasper Kincaid – gunfighter hired by Shepard

Zeb Carver – new stage driver whom Hardin helps

Henry Baskin – man on wagon who was shot

by two outlaws
Jeremiah Baskin – Henry and Hannah Baskin's son
Silas McCready – Corporal fights Blackfeet beside Hardin
Takoda Redleaf – crow Indian tracker for the army
Jedediah Colter – owner of Iron Wheel Express Stage Line
Caleb Driscoll – took hit over the head at Bitterroot Springs
Gordon Slade – rides to find Hardin to stop Cornelius Vance
Silas Granger – trapper #1
Levi Hawthorne – trapper #2
Hoge Finnegan – trapper #3
Thaddeus Boone – rides shotgun for the stage
Darren Marks – brought word to Hardin about hurt man
Rufus Taggart – guest at Faye's boarding house
Virgil Creed – guest at Faye's boarding house
Silas Boone – guest at Faye's boarding house

Female characters

Lydia Travers – waitress at the cafe at Bitterroot Springs

Darcy West – waitress at the cafe at Bitterroot Springs

Victoria Hawkins – doctor who starts a practice at Bitterroot Springs

Sarah Harlan – journalist at the Bitterroot Chronicle

Vera Watts – Faye's friend and guest at the boarding house

Faye Rogers – boarding house owner at Bitterroot Springs

Eleanor Pike – Cactus Bloom Hotel owner at Miles City

Abigail Mercer – female hotel clerk at Miles City

Sarah Holt – Banker's wife at Bitterroot Springs

Rebecca Wightman – Harold Wightman's wife at mercantile

Hannah Baskin – pioneer woman whose husband is shot